ANIMALS
EAT
EACH
OTHER

ANIMALS EAT EACH OTHER

ELLE NASH

DZANC
BOOKS

DZANC
BOOKS

5220 Dexter Ann Arbor Rd.
Ann Arbor, MI 48103
www.dzancbooks.org

Library of Congress Cataloging-in-Publication Data

Names: Nash, Elle, author.
Title: Animals eat each other / Elle Nash.
Description: Ann Arbor, MI : Dzanc Books, 2017.
Identifiers: LCCN 2016039154 (print) | LCCN 2016039627 (ebook) | ISBN
    9781938604430 | ISBN 9781945814075 ()
Classification: LCC PS3614.A727 A6 2017 (print) | LCC PS3614.A727
(ebook) |
    DDC 811/.6--dc23
LC record available at https://lccn.loc.gov/2016039154

First US edition: April 2018
Interior design by Leslie Vedder

Printed in the United States of America

10   9   8   7   6   5   4   3   2   1

There is a cost to being special.
Most people are not willing to pay that price.

—*Wal-Mart Vice President, 2010*

You can run as fast as you want,
but you can never outrun your cliché.

—*Doppelherz, Marilyn Manson, 2003*

PROLOGUE

MATT PLACED THE KNIFE on my face, pressing down against my lips. He wanted me to lick the edge of it, to push my tongue up against the serrated edge so he could watch the way the muscle in my mouth looked against the metal. With his other hand, he held my neck to the floor.

The one who tied me to the coffee table was his girlfriend, Frances. Her hand was on my thigh, small and smooth and birdlike, occasionally caressing back and forth across my leg as I lay on my back, pressed into the living room carpet. Frances was naked and sat with her legs under her, tourmaline hair falling to her lower back. We were drunk again, their baby asleep in his crib in the bedroom down the hall.

I squirmed my hips to get comfortable, inched my head left to keep my hair from pulling. Matt's fingers, thick and callused, wrapped tighter around my neck. The pressure in my skull increased in slow heartbeats, the room fading into an inky black vignette. His eyes, the kind of blue you only see in nature documentaries about very cold places, stared into mine. I stared at the bridge of his nose to seem like I was staring into his eyes. At moments, I would catch his gaze and almost see a flash that I was a Real Living Thing, visceral and bleeding.

I wanted to be validated, the way everyone does. I ended up between a floor and a knife, between a man and the mother of his child. This was before I understood what it was like to be held close, to-the-ribs close. Close like I was the only one.

FROM DUST

THAT SUMMER I WORKED at RadioShack in a dull strip mall, three miles from my mother's place in Lamplighter mobile home park. We moved to Lamplighter when I was eight, after my father died from sudden liver complications, leaving us with a garage-sized inheritance of 1970s knick-knacks, old photos, and debt. My mother was a caretaker for the elderly, and although she worked through most holidays, her income alone couldn't pay the mortgage on the rambler they had bought when they first moved to Colorado Springs.

All summer, my mother had been prodding me to find a job. I'd just graduated high school and had no immediate plans for college, instead investing my time in a growing obsession with snorting Percocet. I was thirteen the first time I thumbed one of my mother's pills, a Vicodin—only one because I feared she might notice it was missing. I remember carrying it back to my bedroom like a fragile tooth, and I placed it under my pillow with the same excitement that used to come from exchanging body parts for quarters. I brushed my teeth and washed my face in the hallway bathroom and when I came back, the pill was still there. I swallowed it with a glass of water, and at first felt very nauseous. Then a warmth spread from my belly into the rest of my limbs and I felt comforted in a way I hadn't in a long time. It reminded me of a moment when I'd woken from a nightmare as a child and crawled into bed between both my parents, cradled by the largeness of their bodies and the smell of their sweat, both sweet and stale like old cigarettes.

Jenny and I stood behind the linoleum counter at the store, waiting on customers. Jenny was a girl I knew from middle school, who had worked at RadioShack since her sophomore year and got me a job, too. The summer had faded into cool evenings on the cusp of autumn, and wispy locks of Jenny's pastel blue-tipped hair fell from her beanie. Poised between the gray squares of economy carpet and the stacked electronics, she was the brightest thing in the store.

That's when Matt and Frances walked in. Jenny took them immediately to the only corner of the store where the camera couldn't see them.

Matt was tall, his head shaved so close to the scalp I could see the lines in his cranium. Frances stood next to him, her fingers wrapped delicately between his own. With her other hand, she held the tips of her long hair to her mouth. She constantly checked the reaction on Matt's face as Jenny spoke to them, as if any move she made or word she said was subject to his approval. Her almond-shaped eyes were exaggerated by her thin, drawn-in eyebrows. Matt pulled out a tube of Chapstick and unscrewed the top. He puckered his lips and put it on, his cupids bow glistening in the dead-pale fluorescent lighting. I stared at his upper lip, the bulge and glow of it, until I heard my name.

"Matt is a tattoo artist," Jenny repeated loudly. I wondered how long the three of them had been watching me. "Show him yours!"

I lifted my shirt to show them the tattoo on my stomach—a barn owl, feathers spread like fingers between my hipbones. I thought about the security cameras and what it might look like if my tiny gray figure lifted her shirt up for a couple of strangers, but since the camera couldn't see them, I hoped it would be innocuous, like flashing a ghost. The tattoo itself was bare, only line work done three weeks ago. It was my first big piece, an impulsive decision after a dramatic summer break-up.

I had other tattoos, smaller ones I didn't show off. At first I was attracted to changing the image of myself, placing tokens on my body to center who I was or where I'd been. After a while, I began to enjoy the dry, dull pain and the way each tattoo forced me to confront my own commitment to be hurt over and over again. The first tattoo, a set of stars trailing down my spine, was the most painful. After the artist inked the first line into my skin, a shroud of dread held me in the chair. I couldn't stop him. If I did, I'd be walking around my whole life with this symbol of weakness etched into my skin. When he dragged the needle down, he focused one hundred percent of his attention on me, and I liked that. The tattoo scabbed over so badly that the color mottled.

After that, I wanted to go bigger, more detailed, in more sensitive places. Cursive words on the backs of my thighs: *hopeless/romantic*. A moon on my ankle, where the skin was so thin the needle felt like splintered toothpicks rubbing frantically against the bone. The decision to get the owl tattooed right on my stomach was physical proof of my control over my body. The wings feathered out toward my hipbones, and the tail pointed down toward the most interesting part of my body, or at least the one that seemed the most interesting to other people. My mother lamented how it might stretch if I were ever to have a child, but I told her I wasn't worried about that. The outline had been excruciating. The closer the artist got to my pelvis, the more I clenched my abs against the pain. I'd made it through the worst of the thick line work; all that remained now was the color.

The next day at work, Jenny told me Matt and Frances were interested in me, like I was a subject to be explored. When I asked what she meant, she simply said, "They want to get to know you more."

A week went by. Jenny gave me Frances's number. I called, a landline. Her voice sounded thick and warm. She asked if I was free that Saturday.

When I arrived, I located the garden-level window of their apartment and checked my phone. I was already ten minutes late.

Their door was hidden from the street. There were nail holes on the doorjamb where the numbers were supposed to be. The frame was a gray muted blue, painted with acrylic, the kind that peels off with age. I placed my index finger against a hole on the hinge side of the door and a paint tag caught underneath my fingernail. The lip of it nudged in between the tip of my finger and the underside of my nail. The feeling of separation, of space between these two minuscule parts of my body, and the gummy yield of the acrylic filled my chest with a sense of relief. I pulled until the tiny string of paint snapped.

Frances opened the door, the light catching her deep brown eyes. "Come in, come in!" she said. She grabbed my hand and pulled me into the house. Her hands were cool and small, like clutching a tiny animal. I felt as if I could squeeze too hard and somehow kill it.

"Hey," I said. "Frances, right?" I tried to smirk, and she smiled back, revealing a slight space between her two front teeth.

"You can call me Frankie," she said.

Up close, Frankie's skin was smooth and almost poreless. She had freckles across her nose and cheeks, and her teeth seemed unnaturally white. My teeth were slightly yellowed and I did too many things to my body that made it feel old and tired, as though I were dragging all of the mistakes I'd ever made behind me with each step.

Frankie closed the door and walked me in. My eyes struggled against the light. The entryway led into the living room, where a baby-blue velvet sofa wrapped around two whole walls, oriented to a wooden entertainment center. A few hand-drawn pieces of art hung framed on the wall; I guessed they were Matt's work. I remember the distinct feeling of their adulthood: a home with furniture, kitchen utensils, bathroom cleanser, a wipe-off calendar. When we'd moved to the trailer, my mother got rid of most of our furniture, and I slept without a mattress for some time. It seemed to take years for us to recollect the things we needed—sharp kitchen knives, a cutting board, a dented saucepan with tarnish crusted around the rim.

Frankie's sparrow hands led me through the kitchen. A stack of old bills, a strangely shaped bag, a napkin holder, and some stains littered the circular dining-room table. A hand-painted glass vase with dried willow branches leaned against the napkin holder. The clutter betrayed the neatness of the rest of the house. She pulled a chair out for me and I sat. Salt crumbs pushed into my elbows when I placed my arms on the table. I looked around. Aside from the high chair, there seemed no other evidence of a child.

"Matt is dropping the baby off at his mom's house." Frankie pulled out a chair but didn't sit. "He should be back pretty soon."

"How old is your baby?" I asked.

I tried not to stare at her body. Although Jenny had said they were interested in me, I didn't want to make the mistake yet of interpreting their friendliness as anything more than curiosity.

"Jett's about ten months old," she said. "He just took his first steps last week."

I didn't know if ten months was an exceptional time to learn how to use your feet to move your body. I stared at her poreless, makeup-free skin, thinking of what to say.

I wondered how she felt about seeing me this close, an arm's length away, where she could see the mistakes in my makeup or the pimples underneath, could smell my breath or skin or hair. I wondered if she felt the same pulse of heat about our bodies, the way I felt it. My hand searched along the bottom of the table for something to pick off, paint or cardboard or wood splinters. When I didn't find anything, I picked at the skin of my thumb.

"Oh," I said. "That must be exciting."

She nodded and smiled. Her eyes lit up affectionately. "He gets more mobile every day. It's always changing," she said.

I wanted to get close to Frankie. I always wanted that with girls, especially when they were older or seemed cooler than I was. I wanted to become her best friend, to feel her from every angle. As a result, I became nervous. I didn't want to fuck it up.

"There's a show tonight," she said. "We can go out when Matt gets back."

"Cool," I said. "Sounds good. How do you two know Jenny?"

"Well, Matt and Jenny go way back," Frankie said. "Knew each other in middle school and everything."

The cuticle of my thumb began to bleed. I nodded.

"I met Jenny when I started dating Matt," she said. "What was that, sophomore year? Or freshman?" She asked as if I would know, like we were longtime friends with an intertwined history. Dust motes circled beneath the overhead light. "God, it's been so long, it's like Matt and I are practically married." She laughed like she was trying to prove something. I laughed, too.

Eight years later, I'll look her up on social media and retrace the constellation of each event. I'll laugh as I scroll through picture upon picture of their life after me—both hers and his, status updates and in her bio: *To have and to hold. Married since 2003, a decade plus of matrimonial bliss.* The year of our life together erased. As if she'd never called me Lilith, like she did the first night she saw me naked. As if nothing I'm about to tell you ever actually happened.

ABSORBED INTO THE BODIES OF MEN

MATT CAME HOME. HE and Frankie stood in the hallway, arms around each other, unmoving. His eyes locked onto mine, and it was like this that I saw something familiar in him for the first time, some flicker that made me burn between my legs. I quickly looked away.

"Hey," he said. "Cool to see you on the other side of the cash wrap." He reached his hand out to me to shake and instinctively I put my hand out, too. What happened when our skin collided is what happens to sweat on a summer body, the way the heat turns everything wet into a hot, sticky vapor. His thumb reached up and over the whole of my hand. I touched him like chalk against a chalkboard, like I could feel each part of me dissolve against his skin. As if I wasn't standing in their front room, shaking hands with a strange man, like this was some job interview to get fucked.

Matt moved out of the entryway and into the kitchen to grab some beers. When he stepped away, Frankie kept her eyes on me. Did she want to be my friend? Fuck me? That was the first time she looked at me as though she might unhinge her jaw and eat me, which was both arousing and unnerving. She grabbed my wrist harder this time and led me back to the kitchen table.

"You want a beer?" Matt asked.

"Anything harder?"

"We don't have any liquor right now," he said. "I can get Patrick to bring some later."

I wondered who Patrick was—a fourth player? Matt's walk to the table was slow, setting Frankie's beer down first, and then mine, next to the one he'd finished. I stared at the bottle and watched the way his hand slid from the neck down the body, gathering the slick condensation.

"So, like, I heard you're a tattoo artist," I said.

"You could say that, yeah."

"What kind of stuff do you tattoo?"

He leaned into the hand pressed down on the table, so his hip jutted out a little, almost brushing me. "Small stuff," he said. "I do it from home."

Frankie pointed to the art on the walls. A screaming mouth that reminded me of *Cool World*. A lot of attempted graffiti, cartoon teddy bears with angry teeth and stoner eyes. The kind of shit every white boy from Colorado Springs drew in high school. I pretended to be impressed.

He was wearing cologne, as though he cared about the closeness of our bodies. It was subtle and understated, like watered-down scotch. "I can tattoo you for free if you want," he said. "Whenever you want."

When I was very little, before my dad died, a cashier at McDonald's asked me if a happy meal on the counter was mine. My family had already gotten their food, so I said no and wandered back over to my table. My father grabbed me by the shoulders and looked me right in the face. His hair was this tousled shoulder-length mane, brown already going gray, and at the time he'd had a mustache. He said, "Whenever someone offers you something for free, you take it." The seriousness of his voice scared me.

I didn't understand yet that desperation was a trade I'd learn, too.

"He doesn't work in a shop," Frankie said. "But we can tattoo you for sure."

She said it again—"we." When couples are together long enough, they speak as though they are one creature. I wondered if that was a thing only women did, as if we were absorbed into the bodies of men, molded inside of them with only the indigestible parts of us left over. I thought of my mother and how unmolded she had become since my dad died.

My first memories of her are as a homemaker. We ate dinner at the dining room table every night. Then my dad would watch TV as she did the dishes. He would complain about the noise of the water and she would bring him a Seven and Seven. After that, we'd all watch *The Simpsons* together before the evening news. His glass would empty and he'd shake it like a Yahtzee cup, the ice rattling around inside. My mother would fill it again, and another time. When the evening news came on, she'd ready me for bed.

After his death, my mom and I ate off TV trays in the living room. We ate microwave dinners, pizza Hot Pockets, and boxed macaroni and cheese. Sometimes she would make Hamburger Helper. She worked a lot of evening shifts. I learned how to unlock a deadbolt and use a microwave. Her weight crept up—rapidly at first, from antidepressants and anti-insomnia drugs, and then later it evened out. If she wasn't working, she was asleep on the couch with the soft glow of the TV on her skin while I sat cross-legged on the floor, eating from a greasy paper plate on the coffee table. Her excess weight led to joint pain, which led to Vicodin and Percocet. Eventually, we stopped eating together.

Matt shifted on his feet and Frankie got up from her seat at the kitchen table.

"I seriously love that tattoo," Frankie said. She came over and lifted my shirt. Matt leaned in to get a better look. "Where did you get it done again?"

"Glory Badges," I touched my stomach protectively. "But the artist who did the outline split. I have to figure something out."

"Shit," said Matt. "That's rough. Maybe I could do the color for you."

"I'll have to think about it," I said.

When I got the outline done, I went back to the empty mobile home and burst into tears. I didn't know if I was crying because it hurt so bad or if I was crying because I had failed by letting the pain hurt me so much. Matt sensed my hesitation.

"I haven't worked that big yet," he said. "But we can bang out something small on you first."

"He's so good." Frankie grabbed a sketchbook and took me over to the couch. "Look at some of this."

The weight of our bodies on the couch pushed us together. I could feel her torso against my own, the light, flimsy fabric of her shirt against my arm. She spread the sketchbook open on both of our laps and flipped slowly through the pages of Matt's sketches. A lot of the pictures were similar to what I saw on the walls, but unfinished. Eventually, she flipped to a page covered with the speckled purple bells of foxglove flowers. They hung heavy and low toward the bottom of the page, with smaller buds toward the top, a thick stem and a few leaves for aesthetic balance. It struck as me as feminine, more so than any of the other half-finished drawings in the book, maybe because it was the most natural and realistic of the drawings.

"This would be so perfect on your skin," Frankie said. "This is so you."

Matt leaned over us. "Oh yeah, that would look good on you."

"I've never done anything like this before," I said. "Not like—a tattoo in someone's house."

"It'll be fun," said Frankie. "Matt tattooed Jenny before. Did you know that?"

Jenny never told me about any tattoo. I wondered what else she hadn't told me.

•

We left their house in one car to go to the metal show. The Black Sheep sat on the border between the rich and the poor part of town, where the drainage in the sewer systems gets bad. We arrived late, and the second band was already playing. The stage was set against the back wall, with a few scratched-up tables and chairs and room for the mosh pit. Matt went to mosh in the pit while Frankie and I sat at a booth near the bar.

"It's nice to be out without the baby," she said.

I fumbled with a pack of cigarettes. She rested her face onto her knuckles, as if she also needed something to do with her hands. Our nervous energy was contained in the ways we kept our bodies occupied. I inhaled my cigarette and blew out, turning my face away from her. I did not know yet what it was like to be needed all the time.

"Is it hard for you, being with the kid all of the time?" I asked.

"It's the treasure of my life," she said, and smiled. I realized she'd had Jett at seventeen. I asked her if she finished school after.

She shook her head. "I'm working toward getting my GED," she said. "And anyway, school didn't work for me. I don't know why. I just didn't care."

I agreed with her, keeping to myself that I had recently graduated with an almost 4.0 average. I offered her a cigarette and she said no. We watched Matt move through the mosh pit, enjoying the music.

Matt's friend Patrick showed up with his girlfriend Maya. He wore a brown bomber jacket, which he unzipped to show us he'd snuck in a bottle of vodka. We all drove to the Satellite Hotel, a brutalist brick building in the shape of a three-armed star. When I was young, I thought it was called the Satellite because the biggest industry in Colorado Springs outside of Jesus was the defense industry, but later

I learned it was because the top of the hotel housed some kind of radio array. The hotel was on the south end of town, near the shitty comedy club. The car rocked over the countless potholes. It wasn't far from Lamplighter. When I was in high school, I would sneak up on the hotel roof with friends and we'd split a handle of Tullemore Dew.

We stopped at a gas station, bought a roll of electrical tape and climbed the stairs of the hotel, eleven flights up with a door that would lock behind us. I pushed lumps of black electrical tape into the hole for the latch bolt, and then taped over it after it was stuffed so we could get back out.

On top of the hotel, we passed the vodka around, the sky as big and wide as I'd ever seen it. I stood a couple feet from the edge of the building, looking out at the city. You could see the cemetery, which in two years would flood from violent summer storms, freeing coffins from their graves. On the corner was the red Conoco and Burger King. Next to that was the strip mall with the liquor store where the clerk got murdered when they turned off all the street lamps due to budget cuts, and the Pentecostal church squeezed between it and Mary's Bar.

Frankie was the first to go toward the edge. There was no railing or lip. It fell like a cliff, and Frankie stood there, looking over it, the wind pushing her dark hair all around her face. She laughed unsteadily, like there was no edge at all. Patrick and Matt sat with their legs hanging off, swinging back and forth. Maya grabbed a bag of chips from her purse and joined them.

Patrick passed the bottle of Burnett's, first to Matt, then Maya and Frankie, and then Frankie reached back to me. I drank long, letting it strip the saliva out of my throat. Instead of walking to the edge, I wormed my way over, crawling like a slug. I was too buzzed to trust my balance. Wind rushed up, flying. They all sat there looking over the void and all I could do was crawl.

IF YOU DON'T LEAVE YOUR HOMETOWN AFTER HIGH SCHOOL, YOU'LL JUST GET BAD TATTOOS AND DO LOTS OF DRUGS

THE SECOND TIME I hung out with Matt and Frankie, the conversation turned to what tattoo I wanted. Matt grabbed some tracing paper and started sketching. Frankie looked up some pictures on the Internet. I already knew I wanted foxglove flowers. Matt and Frankie got to pick where the tattoo went.

Matt got his supplies ready as Frankie set up a chair in the middle of the living room. She kneeled in front of me, unlaced my shoes, and then looked up. She pulled off each of my shoes and reached her hands up to my hips. I stared at her. Her fingers found the button of my jeans and I placed my hand on hers to stop her. She didn't seem afraid to make the first move. I wondered why I was.

"Where?" I asked.

"I'll show you," she said. Matt glanced over, setting out the different colors of ink.

I nodded my head at the living room window, the light, the green grass outside. Frankie got up and turned the blinds. When the direction of the light changed, I saw how the dust lay on every surface in a way I couldn't see before. My mother's house was like this. She hid all the things that made it look dirty but didn't wipe counters or sweep floors. When the light came in, you could see all the spots Frankie had missed, all her mistakes. Then it got darker and the dust disappeared.

Frankie leaned over me again, her hair trailing down like a hand to my throat. She traced her finger along the zipper seam of my jeans.

I thought about Jenny and wondered which tattoo Matt had given her, whether it had happened the same way. Frankie picked her finger up to unbutton my jeans, but before she did I moved my hands and unzipped them for her, pulling them off halfway and revealing my black lace underwear. I'd picked that pair intentionally. She laughed, either at my actions or taste in lingerie, and said to Matt, "You should do her inner thigh." Salt from the table had somehow made its way onto the chair, the grit sticking to the bare skin on the backs of my thighs.

Matt kneeled in between my legs. I'd never had a one-night stand or slept with a stranger, much less two. Most people I'd slept with were in my proximity, like my manager at work, which felt safe because I knew him, but also because of the lack of emotional content. That was how I liked sex to be. Frankie stared from the couch. The plastic latex of Matt's gloves crackled as he put the tattoo gun together and opened a fresh package of needles.

The new needles were a relief. Matt was a stranger to me; I was letting someone I did not know stick needles into my body. I imagined blood particles inside of old needles, dirty needles in dirty skin, needles in other girls or in old men who rode motorcycles who fucked girls like me who got tattoos in someone's apartment. Needles being handled by a man who says "trust me" and so you do.

Matt's foot depressed the pedal on the floor. There was a sudden, familiar sound, an angry rumble. He placed his cold hands on the inside of my knees and pushed my legs outward, parting my thighs. He watched me as I did this and I stared at his third-eye spot.

"Close your eyes," he said.

I closed my eyes.

I liked doing what he told me to do. The pressure of his hands slid down the inner muscle of my thigh. The cloth was cold and smelled sterile, like hospital soap. The tissue paper of the design he drew fell against my thigh and attached hungrily, stuck to me as the purple ink transferred to my skin. Frankie told me I wasn't allowed to look at the tattoo until it was done.

After Matt placed the tracing, the first prick of the needle dragged across my skin. He bent, concentrated on the work, and I resisted the urge to run my fingers along the stubble of his shaved head.

"Where'd you buy your tattoo gun?" I asked.

"Don't call it a gun." His voice was stern, the way he emphasized the word *gun*.

"Yeah," Frankie said. She rubbed her hands on the couch, readjusted her body a bit. She'd been so quiet I almost forgot she was there. "The word gun makes it sound like tattooing is somehow violent."

"Isn't it?" I asked. "Violent, I mean." Matt stretched the skin tight. As he moved up toward the spot where my hip and thigh met, the rawness set in. I felt the skin taut between his fingers, the latex-covered index and thumb of his left hand, the needles in between that skin space.

"Tattooing is an art," he said. "Not marksmanship."

Matt removed the needles for a moment and looked up at me, one eyebrow raised. My skin prickled a little, out of fear or nervousness, or because I was cold and half-naked in someone's chair.

"Guns destroy," he said. "This creates."

He took the damp cloth with the hospital soap smell and wiped off the extra ink. I asked Frankie for my beer and took a swig. I imagined my fingers running across the raised skin, the new scar Matt was creating. When he moved his hands toward my hips, the tattoo burned a sudden hot I couldn't stand. All the crevices of my body sweated as I took another drink of beer. I felt the cold and fizz on my tongue, my damp armpits, and the burn of the alcohol at the back of my mouth.

In pain all senses are heightened. The mind has to go deeper than the immediate to be okay. Pain is a form of meditation that defeats the now. It is not about being present with the pain but being beyond it, being able to breathe and function and think, being able to survive without kicking and screaming.

Matt put the needles back on my skin. I rolled my head back against the chair and raised my arms above my head. I tried to keep my legs relaxed. Every now and then, his hand rested on part of my thigh.

"Do you like tattoo sex?" Matt asked.

"What?" I said.

"Do you like tattoo sex?"

I wondered if he was going to fuck me and tattoo me at the same time. Maybe they were into weird shit like that. Matt's head was down, eyes on the tattoo as he spoke.

"Tattoo sex is when the needle goes in and out," he said. "When the pain feels so good you could come."

I breathed in the skin of my thigh stretched between his forefinger and thumb, breathed in between swigs of warm beer and the pain shooting up from my pelvis. I breathed in between Frankie on the couch, the way she watched over her kingdom, and Matt on the floor. His shoulder bones moved back and forth underneath his shirt, widening and unwidening like the muscles of some large beast.

"Do you like pain?" I asked.

"No," he said. "But I bet you do."

I looked over at Frankie and she smiled.

HOPELESS / ROMANTIC

THE BUZZING WAS IN my head. It was in my bones, my thigh bone, my hips. It was in the chair, threading up my spine. It stayed within me long after he was finally done. Matt wiped away the last of the stray ink with a paper towel. The hospital smell stung my skin and nose. Frankie went back to their bedroom to grab a full-length body mirror. As I stood up and turned around, I knew Matt would see the tattoos on the back of my thighs. He grabbed my hip first, pushing me against the back of the chair, the latex from his glove pulling my skin in a way that hurt. I was a little drunk from the beer but I surrendered in part because my body dissolved again when he touched me. My laugh sounded strange to me, like it was a sound that did not belong to my teeth and tongue once it left my mouth.

"Whoa," he said. "Hang on a sec."

I placed my hands on the back of the chair and straightened my arms, bending over. Matt yelled into the bedroom for Frankie, grabbing my thigh the same way he grabbed my hip, firm. He rubbed the tattoo a little, as if he could feel the ink scars underneath the latex glove. I remembered getting them done, lying on my belly with my arms curled underneath me as the artist worked, and then tracing my fingers over each of the new letters, the ridge of scarring raised gently on the skin.

"Coming!" Frankie yelled back. She lugged a full-length mirror down the hall, my reflection bouncing back and forth in it as she got to the living room. She placed it upright against the couch and let out a heavy breath.

"Okay," she said. "Time to see your new tattoo!" She walked over and stood next to Matt.

"Look at these," he said, motioning to my thighs, the words on them.

hopeless / romantic

I blushed and was suddenly aware of the open air all over my almost naked body. The tattoo itself was more like a wish. I didn't feel connected to anyone in a romantic way, and most of the time sex felt like a stand-in for whatever romance was supposed to be.

When I'd slept with Sam, my manager, I felt detached from the sex even though I harbored a deep longing for his attention. He had a girlfriend; his lack of emotional availability seemed attractive. I wore skirts to work with the intention to seduce him, and after we started to fool around in the store, I shaved my legs every morning. He waited for me to turn eighteen, but even before my birthday we were flirting on the clock. When I woke up at his house one Saturday morning, I realized I felt just as detached from him as from the boy I was currently dating, and that I probably shouldn't be dating anyone at all. I was more attracted to a person's interest in me than to the particulars of their personalities, or the things they liked to eat, or what they liked to do when they weren't texting me or sleeping with me. I left Sam's apartment that morning while he was in the shower, a note on the pillow that said, *had fun! see you at work. xoxo, L*

Sometimes having sex with Sam hurt, in the sense that I would not be quite ready but he would want to start anyway. I would face away from him and he would enter me, and I would feel myself force an acceptance of his presence in my body. It wasn't that I didn't want to have sex; more like, I wanted his attention so badly that I didn't think I could be picky about the type of attention I received. Since I wanted to be an object of his attention, I believed that I also had to be an object of his pleasure.

Often, during sex, it would take me a few minutes to figure out whether something felt good or if it was painful. Eventually, it seemed it was mostly hurting, or that it was fine but I was empty and detached. By then so much time had passed that to stop or readjust felt like breaking an unspoken rule.

I learned to restructure these feelings of pain or detachment into a type of pleasure, and I did this by performing what I thought sounded and looked like a woman enjoying sex so that I wasn't just lying there, emotionless and unmoving. When I was sixteen, I'd heard a phrase at school: *It's like sticking your dick in a coffin.* If I were going to live my life as a receptacle of bodies, I did not want to be a coffin.

Matt cleaned the new tattoo and bandaged me up. I wanted badly to touch it although it was an open wound. My leg felt wide and raw and the purple flowers with its thick green stems looked neon against the redness of my irritated thigh. Frankie moved me to the couch. She slipped my shirt off in the same delicate way she took off my shoes. Her fingers were gentle and cool against my skin as she lifted it up and over my head. My body tensed at the sudden way she moved me, as though I were an art doll or a mannequin. The action of removing my clothes and then placing me on the couch, first my shoulders, then the long line of my back, seemed to come so naturally to her that I thought she had done this before, or that she had done this with other women before without Matt there. Matt was on the other side of the coffee table, standing very still with his arms folded tight against his chest. It was dark outside and the light from the kitchen gave everything a dark desert tinge of yellow.

Frankie put my legs up on the couch. Her fingertips traced their way down my leg like she was studying me through touch. I watched her eyes curve up at the corners as she smiled, the gunsmoke and amber color of her eyes moving from spot to spot on my skin. When she was done, she stood next to Matt, and they both looked at me.

That was when she said it, what made me forget my name.

She said, "She's just like Lilith."

Matt wiped sweat from his forehead and I realized how hot it was. My skin against the velvet couch, the big body of it holding me up.

I lay there, waiting to see what they would do next, which I assumed would involve sex of some kind. I did not know who would start, or if we would start by kissing, or how I should feel. I wondered what they expected me to feel, what they expected from watching a naked girl on their couch, if the naked girl should do anything in particular.

I hoped that kissing Frankie or Matt would make me feel something. I liked the idea of new exceptions to mold myself into. I tensed my neck a bit and looked up in a very unnatural way, the way models pose, because I was worried my face might look strange at that angle. I looked at Matt's third eye spot, and then Frankie's, and moved back to Matt's. He shifted from one foot to the other.

"Oh my god you are," he said. "You are totally her."

Me as Lilith. Me as a whole new thing.

I never knew Adam had a wife before Eve, and never questioned why Frankie and Matt might know who Lilith was. Maybe it didn't matter then; maybe I wasn't supposed to know. Years later, my late-night social media stalking would transition to a drawn-out search for information about Lilith. I learned that Lilith was made from the same dust as Adam, and not from his rib. I learned that Lilith was either banished or left the Garden because she refused to obey, and it seemed likely to me that was why Eve was punished the way that she was, as if any form that was not Adam was set up from the beginning to fail.

I wondered if knowing this would have changed the way I interacted with Matt and Frankie. When Frankie named me, I felt wild and free to her, like perhaps she respected me or saw something exciting in me that I could not see in myself.

Frankie put her hand on my bare leg and left it there. I was on my fifth or sixth beer and it was easier for me to open into the warmth of her palm. I wanted more of her hand caressing my upper thigh. I wanted more beer, and to let go deeper into the warmth of her skin against mine.

Frankie leaned in to kiss me. I closed my eyes. At first, I felt the same emptiness. There was a sense that I was kissing a person, and there was an excitement about our mouths touching, but my mind understood that the feeling was only physical. I reached out to touch her neck and leaned in to kiss her harder. I had seen this in movies, and while it looked very romantic and passionate, mostly I felt her teeth beneath her lips. She moved her hands around my body and then there was another pair of hands. These hands were larger, rougher, and there was a firmness in them like they were corded with muscle. It gave me the distinct feeling of being worshipped. It was more comforting than any I had felt before—sleeping in on Sunday morning in a mess of blankets, snorting Percocet and watching PBS, eating a whole bag of Doritos without having to share. More comforting than memories of my dad. Matt was behind me, and I felt encased, like the yolk of an egg.

Frankie moved her hand to reach inside of me. The sharp point of her fingers was uncomfortable at first. After that first feeling, I seemed to pour into her hands. I attempted to move my hips in a circular motion, to find a pace where things felt good, but her hands were clumsy and it was like she didn't understand what she was touching.

I began to perform for them. I gave moans that seemed believable, and kept rocking my hips in a circular motion. The repetitive motion of sex that sounded like it felt good but felt only half decent reverberated through my mind. The sex became an absurd echo in which I was a caricature of myself.

I focused on the parts that did feel good, like Frankie's lips against mine at that same time as the warmth of Matt's hands enveloped my body, or the feel of his lips and teeth against my neck while he heaved his clothed body against my skin..

That they were both clothed and I was not seemed an obvious barrier, an indication of what my place would be in this relationship. But my performance worked. Frankie's hands were inside me like she wanted to leave something there. I thought about the way Matt's eyes looked up at me when he tattooed me, the needles going in and out of my skin. As he rubbed his hands down my body, I made a high-pitched noise like something in a piano snapping. I didn't say anything. I thought about the tattoo, the needles, his hands stretching and unstretching my skin.

I slowly sobered. I felt cold, and colder still looking at Matt and Frankie fully dressed. When it seemed that Matt and Frankie were not going to remove their own clothes, I eventually pulled away from kissing Frankie. I told them it was getting late.

They seemed surprised that it ended so abruptly. The momentum decayed, and their lack of expectation left me wanting. I no longer knew if I should move the action forward or halt it, or what they had planned for the evening. It seemed ending it would be the right step so they could continue on their own without me.

I stood up from the couch and grabbed my clothes. Frankie smiled at me. I mirrored her warmth because I didn't know what else to do.

"Are you okay?" Frankie asked.

"Yeah—no, I'm good," I said. "It's just I'm tired, I have to work tomorrow, and my mom is probably wondering where I am." The last sentence was a lie, but it sounded plausible.

"Do you need a ride?" Matt asked.

"No, I'll be good," I said.

I pulled on my jeans and buttoned them, and then put on my bra. I lamented the awkward way I always fastened the back of the bra at the front of my chest, before twisting the bra around the right way and then putting on the straps. I wasn't sure if it said anything about my lack of femininity or finesse.

"I appreciate it so much," I added. "I love how warm you guys are. I want to see you again soon."

I paused after putting on my bra, and moved my fingers through my hair, shaking it out.

"God, you're like a wild demon woman," Frankie said.

I did not feel like a wild demon woman at all, but I wanted to come back. I liked the comforting feeling of them on either side of me, but wondered how these two people could find me attractive when I felt such an intense dislike for myself. I questioned it, but I didn't let it hold me back.

When I left, Frankie kissed me on the mouth and Matt hugged me. I thought perhaps me leaving was a good thing, since in a way the evening felt incomplete and it would make them want to see me again.

THE THING ABOUT BOUNDARY ISSUES IS
THAT YOU END UP FUCKING YOUR FRIENDS
OR MAYBE EVERYONE YOU KNOW

ALTHOUGH I HAD ALREADY been sleeping with Sam for a few months, I still felt an intense need for his continuous approval. It got worse when I noticed he had also been flirting with Jenny, which I couldn't get mad about since no one really knew about our arrangement. One night he invited both of us to a midnight pool party at his apartment complex. I showed up alone, in the hopes that everyone else might go home early so Sam and I could have sex.

I recognized a couple of kids I worked with, along with some of Sam's older friends. The summer night was hot and dry in a way that made the sky feel wide open. People splashed each other in the dark, drank PBR. Everyone wore underwear or nothing at all. I opted for a new blue bathing suit with gold trim and a ruched top that I bought from Wal-Mart, but I barely went in the water because my tattoo was still healing. I crossed the pool quickly toward a cooler to grab another beer and felt something brush against my ankle. A hand wrapped around it and tugged me back. When I turned to look behind me, Sam bobbed his head above the water, spitting air and smiling.

"I thought you were a monster," I said.

He swam closer to me. Swirls of water moved across my legs.

"Maybe I am."

Sam tugged at my swimsuit bottoms, his skin shining wet in the streetlights. Sam was twenty-six but already had a bit of a beer gut. His face was young-looking and cute, a little round, and it made him seem approachable. He grew his beard out sometimes in a scruffy way. I felt drugged by his charm, or I felt drugged by my desire for his attention. It was hard to tell which.

He moved closer and I looked around for Jenny. I wondered if they had slept together at all, or if she sensed that there was something going on between me and Sam. I didn't want to hurt her feelings, but it seemed important that Sam pay attention to me, not her, while we were both here and hardly clothed. Jenny was swimming away from us, toward a corner of the pool.

What I did then is what I continued to do for years. I chose sex. I chose validation, attention, over any actual chance at love from friends or even boyfriends. Sam pushed his body against mine. His hands kept tugging at my swimsuit, and he started kissing my neck. I kissed him at first, thinking that we would be shrouded by the darkness of the night, but I hesitated at the thought of Jenny or other coworkers seeing us. He didn't seem to care.

"Come on," he said. I put my hand in his and tried to swim over to the edge of the pool, worried about the water affecting the scab of my tattoo.

"We should go shower first," I said. I picked at the soggy skin on my thumb and it bled a little.

Some of the kids followed us back up to Sam's apartment to get more beer, Jenny too. They sat around finishing off the beers and watched South Park on TV. Sam looked over at me and I looked him.

I walked into his bathroom, waited for him to follow, and turned on the shower. It was clean, with minimal clutter on the countertops and a spotless shower. I saw a spritz of toothpaste spit on the mirror, but that was the only evidence the bathroom was even used. I felt dirty by comparison. I wondered if this was why I wanted him so badly.

Sam walked in and closed the door behind him. He looked me up and down, my skin cold from the wet fabric, and I peeled off my bathing suit, throwing it onto his floor with a thick flop. Sam got naked, one leg out of his swimming trunks and then the other. He stood there, ready, hands at his sides. I stared at his body for a while, watched his beer gut breathe, moved my eyes down his legs and back up to his broad chest and shoulders. He was different from Matt, who seemed feminine, thin and pale in comparison. I didn't make eye contact. Eye contact made things too real.

Water dripped from his hair onto his skin. He got in the shower first. When I stepped in, his hand wrapped around the back of my neck and pulled me in.

This time, the sex didn't hurt. I wasn't focused on moaning or making noises. Other people were in the apartment. He kissed me hard, and then I turned around. I felt him enter me, and I pushed my hands against the tile. My waterproof mascara ran, and my hair was stringy and tangled, astringent from the chlorine of the pool. I did not look my best but he wanted to have sex with me anyway. I felt close to him in that moment.

I heard later that Jenny became very quiet and her face got red at the sound of our skin slapping together in the shower. I imagined her there, wet bleach-blond hair down to her shoulders, wrapped in a towel on the couch, wringing the plastic grocery bag with her clothes in it.

I felt an unusual sense of pride at my ability to emotionally detach from all this. When I had sex with Sam, I didn't feel bad about how Jenny felt. In my journal that night, I wrote:

This time, I am not the dumb girl. I am the smart girl. Jenny is the dumb girl because she let or is letting her dumb feelings get the best of her. She told another coworker, and I quote, "I think I'm falling for him." DO NOT TRY THIS AT HOME. Getting attached to someone is not good.

I brought a half gallon of vodka to her house, where she lived in her parents' basement. By the time a third of the bottle was gone, I grabbed her hand and put it to my mouth, sucked on the web of skin between her thumb and pointer finger. It had been three weeks since that night at Sam's pool.

I stopped in her basement bathroom and caught a glimpse of my face in the mirror. I had recently pierced my septum to match Matt's. I liked the look, and he often hid his piercing, and it felt nice having this mark of pain on my body I could also hide. My eyeliner was thick and drunksmudged. I weighed ninety-three pounds, too skinny to be voluptuous. I smiled at myself, attracted to my image. When I left the bathroom, I wanted Jenny to feel the same way.

I sat close to her on the bed and put my mouth to her neck. My mouth made the shape of a kiss at first and then I held her neck close, bit down. She moaned and I kept going. I pulled her shirt off. I sat on top of her and felt the round of her belly with my hands. She was soft. She laughed, and for the first time I felt unjudged. I grabbed my coffee mug of vodka and Cherry Coke from her nightstand and took a deep sip, the drink dripping from my mouth and falling onto her. I licked them off, and her hands, grasped tight onto my thighs, gripped harder as she arched her back.

I don't remember the rest. We woke up with matching bite-shaped bruises on our bodies: neck, thighs, one on my waist, on her lower back. Our arms were crisscrossed on top of each other, a tangled snake of blanket around us. I stared at the rafters and wondered whether last night was something I could achieve without being under the influence of alcohol. There was an inhibition in me, a fear of my own desires or perversions, that dissolved when I'd had enough to drink or when I mixed my drinks with my mother's pills.

The sunlight painted the white walls pink as it rose through her garden-height windows. We ate bagels with thick cream cheese and left crumbs in her bed sheets and I could hear the sounds of someone, her parents or sisters maybe, stirring milk and sugar into mugs, spoons clinking against ceramic. The smell of coffee wafted down from the kitchen. Jenny's naked leg was slung over me, smooth. Her skin moved against the cactus pins of hair grown out on my own leg. I needed to shower.

She lay on top of the blankets on her stomach, and I noticed a small black tattoo on her lower back—some Chinese symbol. I thought about Frankie saying she'd tattooed Jenny, but was too afraid to ask. Jenny normally wore glasses, but in this moment, she wasn't wearing any. Her eyes were the disturbing color of an afternoon storm gathering in the sky.

I ripped off a piece of bagel and tried to stuff it in her mouth. She jerked her head back, her nose and mouth scrunched up in a smile as she laughed. Her teeth were wide and white. I wondered if I could be closer to Jenny. The parts I did remember felt like safe and sure, even now that I'd sobered up. It took me a few moments to work up the courage to say something to her.

"I was a bitch and I'm sorry," I said. "About Sam, and stupid shit at work."

She stopped smiling. "I was so embarrassed about the pool thing," she said.

"Sam is just like that."

Jenny asked me if I'd spent time with Matt and Frankie yet and I told her I had. I told her about how they had undressed me, but not themselves.

"Frankie seems really into you," she said. "She texted me about how cute she thinks you are."

I had worried that leaving before the sex got more involved might have made me look like a prude. Jenny's assertion made me think it had left them wanting more.

"Oh my *god*," she said. "I have an idea." She spoke excitedly, grabbing my hands like we were old friends. "Dude," she said. "We should fuck with Sam."

I still wanted Sam's attention. I figured this could work in my favor. There were so many times Sam would invite me over, but when I showed up, the house was crowded with other people. Sex with Sam involved a lot of waiting. Sometimes he would say he was tired and go to bed, and I'd leave wondering if I'd done something wrong. Sometimes he would invite me or Jenny over on separate nights, and when we texted him for more details, he wouldn't respond. The next day at work, he acted like nothing had happened.

I crawled across Jenny and grabbed my phone from the floor, flipping it open.

"Think about it," she said. "Who is the real enemy here? We don't need to play games with each other."

I pulled up Sam's number on my phone.

"We should get him to sleep with us," I said. "Like, together."

Jenny threw her head back and laughed. "Holy shit, yes."

"What should I say?"

"Tell him we fucked."

I wondered if Sam would tell the assistant manager, Daniel, about Jenny and I having sex, and about us proposing this three-some, to try and seem cool. I wondered if Jenny was using me to get Sam to like her.

I texted Sam anyway.

He responded back, almost immediately:

—*Nice.*

"That's it?" Jenny bit her bottom lip, pulling the skin back. "Tell him we fucked last night and next time we want *him* to join."

I clasped my phone close to my chest and laughed, hard and nervously. Jenny's attitude was audacious. I wanted to move in closer, to feel her hair against my skin or hands again.

"Okay, okay, okay," I said. "Hang on." I clicked away at my phone, sent the message, and we waited.

No answer.

By the time I went home, he still hadn't responded.

Sam's shift started the same time as mine. I was in the break room getting ready when he walked in, clean-shaven as normal, his shirt untucked. He let the door close behind him and started tucking the shirt into his pants. I instinctively turned away, as if this were a private act and I had never seen him dress or undress before.

Sam scoffed. At work, our relationship was different. It was harder for me to be forward with him, but I hadn't considered whether it was because I was usually sober at work or because there were more cameras and people around. When he was done tucking his shirt in, he moved toward me and I moved away, keeping space between us. It put me into the corner of the break room where the security camera couldn't see. He closed that space and pushed up against me, pushed his body against my body and grabbed my ass. I thought about how, just a few weeks prior, he had led me to a part of the sales floor without cameras and coaxed me into giving him head. I wondered how far he would go this time. His breath smelled like toothpaste, like he'd just woken up, but it was two o'clock. He leaned into me and said, "I'm in."

"Me and Jenny?" I asked.

The door opened. Sam jumped away with his hands behind his back. It was Daniel, the assistant manager. Daniel ran his fingers through his hair nervously. His eyes moved between Sam and me and stopped at the air between us.

"Customers," he said.

I looked at the floor. In my periphery, I saw Sam do this thing with his head, a nod. Daniel closed the door and we were alone again.

Sam put his hands in his pockets, shoulders up to his ears, and walked away. When he got to the door, he looked back at me.

"Yeah," he said. "Friday."

The rest of the day, Sam was more quiet than usual. He also didn't mention Friday again, even when Jenny and I were in the same room or working the same shift. On Thursday, though, Jenny was at the register and I was stocking shelves when Sam walked out of the back room. He stopped, like he forgot we were both working that day. There were no customers in the store. Jenny and I both looked at him, and this wide, stupid smirk spread across his clean-shaven face. None of us said anything.

I considered the mechanics of a threesome with Sam and Jenny. Who would kiss whom first? What would I do if Sam was penetrating Jenny, and would Jenny be doing anything with me? Matt and Frankie's attention that first night had triangulated on me, and while it felt like there was considerable pressure to perform for them, it was easy because I was the object being acted upon and the object against which their desires were playing out. If Jenny and I were actually to sleep with Sam, I wondered if she or I would be more dominant, who would get penetrated first, and whether this weird sexual politicking would feel good or if it would become very awkward afterward. I wondered if the feeling that I was both competing with Jenny for Sam's attention and also with Sam for Jenny's attention would leave me unable to act at all. Or perhaps the solution was simply to drink a lot, take a few pills, and let it all play out as chill as humanly possible.

I'm not really sure why we thought proposing a threesome would be some kind of revenge. After all of the time I spent waiting for Sam to validate me, I think I wanted to finally say to him, *Look what we can do to you. And look how easy it is to get you to do this.*

THERE IS A COST TO BEING SPECIAL

ON FRIDAY, FRANKIE SAID she wanted to play a game, which was unusual. She asked if she could come over to my place.

"I want to play dress-up," she said.

Frankie had asked to see my place before. I was hesitant, in part because my mother had become reclusive since we moved to Lamplighter. If she was home, she was either completely overwhelming in her desire to host, bringing my friends slices of American cheese and Ritz stacked on paper plates with cups of soda, or she would be entirely motionless, slumped on the couch watching whatever was on the TV, Dr. Phil or Judge Judy or the evening news.

Playing dress-up seemed innocuous. When we arrived, my mother's car was gone. Frankie unbuckled the baby from the back-seat of the car and carried him on her hip as she followed me up the wooden porch. Jett hardly looked like Matt's child, except for his lips. He had the same pouty lips, only smaller. Mostly he looked like his mother. He smiled and flapped his arms at me, gurgled in a strange language. He seemed to like my attention, and I was happy to oblige. As we walked into the house, Frankie spoke again.

"The caveat," she said, "is that we're going to go to Wal-Mart in whatever outfit I pick for you."

My hairs rose on my arms. I felt tricked, but I didn't want to tell Frankie no. I wondered what sort of outfit she had in mind for me.

The trailer was dark. I turned on the light in the hallway that led to my room, which felt foreign since I had been spending so much time away from it. My closet was a mess. I sat on the unmade bed, holding Jett in my lap. Frankie began throwing clothes out of the closet and rummaging through a laundry basket of clean clothes on the floor.

"Are you always this disorganized?" she asked.

"I haven't been home in a while," I said, although the state of my room was pretty typical. I had two perpetual piles of clothes on my floor, clean and dirty, and hardly ever wore anything hung up in my closet. I surreptitiously kicked the trash back under my bed, empty soda bottles and candy wrappers.

Frankie had me try on a few pairs of short shorts and a dress before she settled on a pinstripe miniskirt that I'd bought from a cheap, fast-fashion retailer and never wore. She managed to find the one water bra I'd owned in high school, buried at the back of my closet. She dug out a cropped striped polo and a pair of industrial goth platform boots. When she was happy with the outfit, I looked in the mirror. It didn't seem so bad, even if the skirt was pretty short.

The Wal-Mart parking lot looked busy.

"Now for the last touches," Frankie said. She pulled a leather dog collar and a chain leash from her purse. I looked at the collar and then at the baby in the backseat. Frankie fastened the heavy collar around me, the cold metal slicking along my skin.

Frankie pushed the cart with baby Jett in it, holding the leash in her right hand. I walked in front of them. It felt like a parade.

"I need milk," she said. "Get me milk."

I walked in front of her, the weight of the leash swinging behind me, heading for the milk. I picked it up, put it in the cart, and then looked to her for her next command.

People stared. Some shook their heads in disbelief. No one approached us or said anything. A part of me was aroused by the excitement, but my face burned every time I made eye contact with someone. It was easy to do what she said, but I was praying that my mother, or Sam, or someone from high school would not be here to see me. My mind was fighting it. *You just have to do this,* I told myself. Her approval was more seductive than my shame.

Frankie seemed oblivious to the people watching us. Once her shopping list was finished, she walked me to the lingerie section and told me to get on my hands and knees. I looked at her pleadingly.

"Don't you like me?" she said.

"Of course, but I—"

"No one is watching," she said. "If you really like me, you'll do this."

But people were watching. A feeling pressed up into my chest from my stomach. I didn't want to disappoint her.

I got on my hands and knees between towers of socks and hosiery, the industrial-grade carpet flat and hard beneath my palms. She left Jett in the cart and stood behind me with the leash. I could see both of our reflections in a garment mirror. The low thud in my chest seemed to grow louder as pressure built in my head, as if my body was trying to suffocate itself. I struggled to catch my breath. A few people turned their heads toward us. She looked down at me, grinning from ear to ear.

"Now, walk!" she said.

I started to crawl forward like an animal. The tough carpet scraped my knees. I watched the faces of other people. I didn't look like them. They all looked the same—clean, happy. I felt vulnerable and sad and empty, even as I was satisfied that I was brave enough to do what Frankie wanted. All I could think about was how I was not like these people, and how that was bad. I wanted to feel part of something. I wanted Frankie to like me so badly. I was ready to mold myself into what she wanted. The glee with which she enjoyed my humiliation was frightening and felt cruel, but it was hard to discern whether it was truly meant to be cruel or just playful. She was not afraid to demand what she wanted, and I envied that. I spent so much of my life doing what everybody asked me that I wasn't even sure what I wanted anymore, if I wanted anything, if I had needs at all.

Later that night, I brought a duffel bag of different outfits with me to Jenny's house, as well as makeup and a curling iron. Jenny poured me a glass of vodka and Cherry Coke and we drank as we tried on different outfits. I felt almost bored with playing dress-up after what had happened earlier that day.

She wore a bra and panty set I recognized from the lingerie section at Wal-Mart. The lace appliqué on the cups had worn down and was coming off a little. She tried on three different skirts, throwing each of them onto the mess of her floor. We were listening to a CD I made for the summer, a mix of late '90s and early 2000s hip hop in between some top forty songs. I listened to that mix on repeat for so long that even now listening to those songs brings back the smell of Cherry Coke and the feeling of standing in Jenny's room, trying on our clothes.

Her body was wide and sleek like a satin ribbon. Pelvic bones thrust out from her hips, which were the same width as her shoulders. As she twisted, admiring herself in the mirror, the ribbon of her body bent one way and then the other. She bit her bottom lip like she were about to say the word *fuck*, like she was thinking about how good she looked, or maybe how bad. She got on her hands and knees and rummaged through piles of clean and dirty laundry before picking up a pair of tight black jeans and a white T-shirt.

"Maybe simple is better?" she asked. "Jeans or skirt?"

She brought the jeans to her nose and sniffed them before putting them on, one leg at a time, and then threw the T-shirt on, which messed up the plop of dusty blond hair that sat in a bun on her head.

Since we had slept together, I felt more comfortable around her, and less like I had to perform for a stranger who had certain expectations of me. I posed in front of the mirror and shook my hips to the rhythm of the music. She made kissy faces at me, and then at herself, at our reflections dancing in the mirror.

This was the kind of relationship I thought I'd have with Frankie. Jenny was not examining the parts of me, either in whole, seeing me naked, or in pieces with her hands inside of me. Jenny simply experienced me and allowed me to be experienced. Spending time with her was a release from the pressure that had built up with Matt and Frankie. I wondered why I wanted to spend time with them so badly, until I remembered the egg feeling, being encased between their bodies.

I felt like I could trust Jenny. I wanted to tell her about the Wal-Mart incident, but worried she might judge me for being weak or weird.

We danced for a while before I stopped to take another sip. The more we drank, the more Jenny would fall into me, grabbing the soft, exposed parts of my body.

At eight, we both texted Sam, asking him when we should come over. I laid down on her bed and we talked about work. I thought about sharing with her my anxiety surrounding who would do what tonight, and when, and in what positions. Still, I didn't want to come off as weak by revealing my fears. I liked that things felt easy with her, and so I talked around my fears instead, asking her what she thought we would do. We discussed things like *Is he just going to hand me off and then start on you* and *How do you get a blowjob from two girls at once.* We laughed nervously as we discussed each potential situation, and then I realized that we had not heard from Sam all day. I wondered if he would disappear, and in a way I felt a sense of relief.

At ten, we texted him again. Still no response. By then we were both hammered. We'd listened through my whole CD a half dozen times and settled on our outfits and to pass the time we watched *The Hunchback of Notre Dame* on her tiny TV.

There is a fear that comes with opening yourself up like that, even when it is just sex. The moment Sam was pulling at my hips in the pool, I felt every eye on me waiting for me to perform. It was why I tugged him out of the pool, why he followed me into his bathroom and into the shower. There was a natural desire to only be seen by each other.

It's easier than a threesome. Three people observing and experiencing a situation make what's happening more true than if it's just between two. What happens between two people stays between them, and there are only two truths. In the shower after the pool party, there was Sam's version of events and there was my version. The truth cannot be known by anyone other than the person who experienced it. Add a third person, and you get much, much closer to it.

SOLVE ET COAGULA

AT SOME POINT AFTER Matt tattooed me, he let me borrow the autobiography of Marilyn Manson. On the cover is a picture of Manson with an overlay of ribs from a medical book. At the time, *The Golden Age of Grotesque* was only two years old. The album was inscribed with the Waffen-like double M's that had become emblematic of the current iteration of his work. Matt had those double M's tattooed on his bicep. I would see them, myself underneath him, and rub the blank ink with my thumb in the same way that he had rubbed the ink on the back of my thigh.

A week after the Wal-Mart incident, we were all hanging out at their apartment. Frankie was making dinner, the baby was napping. Matt and I sat on the couch, alone for the first time ever. My time had either been spent with both of them together or with Frankie alone. This was the unspoken arrangement of the relationship. I did not know how I should act with just Matt. He wanted to discuss the details of Manson's book with me, of which I had already read about half.

"Manson is a Satanist," he said.

"What does that even mean?"

I had never met any Satanists, though I had been accused of being one in high school many times. I didn't know much about Christianity, despite the religious nature of our town. But Matt called himself a Satanist, too. He had also suggested I get the Satanic Bible.

He said something about religion being an opiate, how everyone in Colorado Springs was just following rules for the sake of following them, and how Satanism was somehow an answer to break free from these constraints.

"It's an antidote," Matt said. "A rejection of the puritanical world that is always pulling you outside of yourself and asking you to serve others shamefully. Always asking you to turn the other cheek."

Frankie clinked dishes in the kitchen, but she couldn't see us. I found it hard to concentrate on what Matt was saying because I was so focused on the novelty of our privacy. I inched closer to him, but it felt wrong somehow. Although Frankie and I were allowed to spend time together, it seemed like she might be upset by me and Matt being close.

"Would you prefer serving shame*lessly*?" I asked.

"Maybe if you did," he said.

He grabbed his own copy of the Satanic Bible from a bookshelf. I noticed words tattooed on the sides of his forearms but couldn't catch what they said.

"Do you know what the Baphomet is?" he asked. I shook my head. He pointed to the image on the cover of the book. It was glossy black, and in the middle was this red-pink pentagram with the tip of the star pointing down, toward the earth. In the star was the image of a goat head.

"Inscribed on his arms are the words *solve* and *coagula*," Matt said. He raised his arms into a prayer position so I could read his forearms, where the same words were tattooed. "It means to dissolve and come together."

I thought about it for a second. I thought about blood, and bodies and blood, and how the coming together of different meats and textures created a human body and then a human brain. How the leap from primordial soup was a kind of coagulation, reaching back to spores and algae. Life was a kind of summoning. Sex was a kind of summoning too, a coagulation of fluids from two people to create another tiny person, the way my parents had created me and so on. I thought about the word *dissolve* and how bodies decayed all the time, the way my father's liver had decayed, and how my mother's body was slowly rotting now, and how I might also be decaying. Every pill or drink I took was a tiny death. I thought about how entropy seemed to be the natural state of the universe. How everything was coming apart, all the time, while also desperately trying to stay together.

"That's basically every force in life," I said.

"The Baphomet scares people because of that," he said. "Everyone has this demi urge to destroy and to create." He moved his face closer to mine. His eyes got really serious and he talked in a low voice. "The darkness inside of them that wants to destroy, to do the bad thing, that wants to serve themselves over others. Everyone has it."

"Is that why I'm here?" I asked. "Are you serving yourself?"

"What I'm telling you is that wanting to serve yourself isn't a bad thing," he said. "Frances was feeling isolated being a new mom. But it's also a way for all of us to push our boundaries a little, don't you think?" he added.

I wondered if Frankie had decided that she needed companionship, and why that companionship had to include sex. At the same time, I had never been very close with any girls in my life unless I was also trying to sleep with them. I think it was less a tendency to sexualize every relationship and more that straight women did not understand me. I naturally disconnected from them. I wondered if this was because sex, that coagula, was the real undercurrent of life. Maybe I had to be sexually attracted to someone to bother spending time with them. Or maybe I craved a tenderness that could only be traded through opening up and sacrificing the vulnerability of my body to another human being. A kind of closeness that I could get from only one other place, a place that disappeared the day my mother became a widow and retreated into herself.

I often felt my presence on Earth served as a daily reminder to my mother that the man she loved so dearly was dead.

Matt sat so that our legs were touching on the couch. Frankie continued to clean in the kitchen. She might walk in and end this short moment we had. His face was close to mine. The heat of his breath emanated between us. He moved his mouth to my ear.

"That's how black magic scares people," he said. "When people come into contact with the things that allow you to communicate with that dark part of yourself, it puts a fear in them. A holy fear. Why do you think Christians fear it so much?"

"I don't know," I said. I thought back to the times I went to church, which was not that often. "Do they?"

"Because they are lying to themselves!" Matt said. "That's all god is anyway, a lie you tell yourself that you're good and wholesome. Everyone is bad. Everyone. And the world is so fucked up because people aren't willing to accept that being bad is a natural thing humans do. They are all just playing a game, where they're lying to each other constantly until they die, because they are afraid."

I was less interested in the religious aspect of his motivations and more interested in this dark space inside of him that seemed to assume the worst in everyone. Was I bad, too? I wondered what he thought of my motivations to be here, and of his own motivations, if he was the one who wanted to open their relationship up more than Frankie.

"So what of it," he said. "Are you afraid?"

The whisper sent an electric pulse through my body, raising all the hair on my skin. My mouth went dry and my hands felt numb. I thought about the way Frankie pulled me through the apartment for the first time, how her eyes watched every movement I made. I wondered if she was also as nervous but had sequestered the feeling within herself. The authority with which she wanted me to do things, and how I followed—the way she gleaned pleasure from my embarrassment. She really did enjoy me, so long as I did what she said. I feared her authority, how sure she was of herself.

That was the fear I had. I didn't know if it was holy.

FROM FEATHERS

FRANKIE HAD BEEN CALLING me Lilith since the first night I came over, since the night Matt grabbed the words *hopeless* and *romantic* on the backs of my thighs with his thick hands. She said it when she tied me up, whispered it to Matt when she told him what to do. Like a pet name, as though this were part of what being loved felt like.

I was a pet though. It is important to remember that. What it means to be chosen first is different—to be under the arms of someone, close to the ribs. Right up next to the chest, but not in the heart. Lilith, a pet who isn't from the body of man. Every time Frankie said it, I believed it a little bit more. I started to be it, started to be Lilith, whoever she was. Something about me slipped away, a letting go. *Lilith*. Each moment the name left her mouth, I liked to imagine I was someone or something else, a hard candy softening my edges against each curl of her tongue. I imagined myself disappearing granule by granule into the pores of her body. Whenever she tied me up and watched as Matt entered me, she watched as though I were a flower, something delicate to be seen and smelled and caressed, and every time he entered me, I didn't need to see myself in the reflection of his eyes. I could only see him and Frankie, myself an object to bring them pleasure. Benign neglect, how peonies thrive.

Frankie was in charge. She dreamt up the world and the world complied. I liked it. Frankie was the center of the mandala, turning us around her. She was always holding my hand, letting me let go a little more each time, into a new me. Frankie didn't name me Lilith because it was who she wanted me to be. She named me Lilith because it was what I wanted to become. I wanted to know what it would be like to carry a bad habit all the way through.

I think Frankie knew it would happen, that my presence would disrupt the daily harmony of their lives in a way that was out of her control. She may not have known when it would happen, but she knew that it could.

Matt and Frankie took me on a ride up to Gold Camp Road in Matt's brand-new Chevy Malibu. We stopped at a gas station first and grabbed snacks, bottles of Diet Mountain Dew and ropes of beef jerky. I got ranch-favored sunflower seeds even though, after a few dozen, the ranch dust flavor started to taste like vomit. I would eat them until the tip of my tongue split with tiny blisters.

Matt loved his Malibu. Slate gray, leather interior, always vacuumed clean unlike my own trashy car. I found the cars of men to be fascinating. There was so little else they seemed to consume in this way in comparison to women—I collected clothes in big heaps and then grew tired of them, but hung on to them as sort of prize. The same with makeup, some of which I'd had since I was nine years old, some I inherited from my mother, makeup kits with bright pink blushes so old the powders became rocks, hardened with talc. Cars were utilitarian but also revealed something about the person with the keys. How deep and low the engine growled, how nice the rims looked, how smooth the gears shifted from third to fourth or fifth. The Malibu was a subtle expression of Matt's personality I came to admire, and by extension Frankie's, since she, too, was associated with the car. We rode around listening to Marilyn Manson on repeat.

Frankie flipped around from the front seat and said, "Do you like this song, Lilith?" playing "Mobscene." She pressed a button to skip to the next track, "Fight Song." She asked over and over again, "Do you like this song, Lilith?" and sang all the words. She turned on the dome light, making the dark outside impossible to see, flipping around every time she asked a question so she could look me in the eyes. I felt the aesthetic of the word each time it left her lips, imagined the supple ways her tongue touched the roof of her mouth or the top row of her perfect white teeth: *Lilith*. How much it carried while being so effortless.

I practiced my trick again, the third-eye spot. Frankie said the name at the end of every sentence: *Lilith, Lilith, Lilith*. I felt like a foreign reactionary playing spy. I wondered if she'd heard Matt and I talking about Satanism in the living room, if I had overstepped. Maybe she saw that I could get too close to Matt, too close to her family. I could get too close and that was why she named me *Lilith*. A girl invited from the dirt of Frankie's private Eden, Frankie whose life was so entwined with Matt's that she came from the bent rib of her lover. Perhaps Frankie was not devoured by the man of her life the way my mother was; it was that she came from him, saw herself as part of him, was so sturdy in his skeletal embrace that she, at first, saw no threat in opening their tannic hearts to me. Lilith was a separate being. That was what Frankie wanted: to close me out. The sinews of their courtship threaded so tightly together that I was merely present to play harp on the tendons of their singular body.

I didn't know all the words, but I tried to play along as best I could. Every time she flipped around, all hair and eyes, fingers gripped to her seat, I'd force a smile. I'd crinkle my eyes, squint them just a bit to make it seem real, and put sunflower seeds in my mouth, wishing they were Percocet.

Where I seemed to fit in with them was wherever Frankie put me. Frankie was the one who tied me to the coffee table with Matt's never-worn ties. Frankie was the one who tied a blindfold over my eyes, who brought me another beer and another, who felt up my thighs with her tiny bird hands. Who whispered to Matt what he should do to me. I mean, I wasn't getting drunk for nothing. I felt so lonely during that whole process. I didn't know who I was becoming at that moment, and because of that, I latched onto whoever I could and molded myself into what they wanted. It was the path of least resistance.

I had been having problems with my birth control, which became apparent a couple of months into my relationship with Matt and Frankie. My period would come for twelve or seventeen days in a row, and then it would go away and come back again with no warning whatsoever. I was taking the pill every day, but after bleeding for ten days I decided to quit all together. I told Matt and Frankie about this, and we resorted to using condoms.

I would still bleed at random, most often during sex. Matt did not seem put off by this at all, and neither did Frankie.

At first, I felt unattractive and dirty leaving stains, and the extra step of having to put a towel down was not conducive to my illusion of sex as an extraterrestrial timeless world in which only we few existed. The bleeding would come unannounced, without pain or cramps, and sometimes mottled brown rather than the attractive deep red color that blood generally was. Frankie constantly reassured me that she didn't care, and I thought both Matt and Frankie's casual disregard for the nature of my body was because she was a mother. Despite being uncomfortable, it felt better to sleep with them than to worry about being rejected by someone else.

We had developed a routine. The arrangement would generally begin with Frankie and I fooling around. We would kiss, and then she would touch me, either with a toy or her hands, and then she would kiss Matt. Sometimes she would tie me up, and then Matt would penetrate me first while Frankie watched. She would hold my hand or keep her hand on my thigh. I was usually on my back, facing away from him.

The first time he choked me, it was unexpected. His hand cupped my neck, and as he enclosed his grip at the highest point of my throat I could feel the pressure of him harden within me. This excited me more than the choking itself, so I didn't protest. He thrusted more vigorously, and as pressure built inside of my head, I imagined my face growing beet-colored and froggy as he finally came. He seemed satisfied with himself, and I wondered if he mistook my open mouth as a sign of pleasure rather than a need for air. I know that humans are animals, but in those moments it seemed that the animal inside him was closer to the surface. I wondered if the animal inside of him was more carnivorous than most. Inside of his eyes, there was a wild pale blue like a wolf on a hill at dawn. His gaze was unnerving, and if I caught it in the right moments, I felt like a kind of prey.

His sex with Frankie was gentler. He regarded her with a tenderness normally reserved for injured animals or children.

At times, sex between us would be so vigorous that I would bleed and something in Matt's face would change. One time his eyes went mannequin blank, glossy and dark, as if the very spirit of his life had escaped him. It was either at the moment of his orgasm or just before. His eyes rolled into the back of his head in the same way that mine did when he choked me, like he was making an attempt to look in on himself and see what was contained within. Matt had just shaved his head again, a soft sort of Velcro blond. My fingers pressed into the muscles of his shoulder and slid up through his hair and bent his face toward my chin. I felt the sharp strain of tendons in my neck against his teeth. He let go and looked at me. I was reminded of the way snorting painkillers feels. A warm bloom began in the center of my head, in the sinus cavity, before spreading like wet, warm fruit smashed under something heavy and hard.

There was the dissolving body feeling and the sharp pain of teeth and the thrust of Matt inside of me all at once. The force of hands holding me down. Something spilled from my middle as if I were splitting in two. Matt pulled out of me and said *blood* and grabbed me harder, grabbed the skin on my waist with his fingertips so hard it left small half-moon scars from his fingernails. Some small tug of my heart pushed words into my mouth, asking *hit me* or *harder*, only for the hope and trophy of a bruise that might form the next day.

I forgot Frankie was there, grabbing my thigh. She'd often place her hands over the wings of the owl tattoo until the presence of her touch dropped off my body like melted wax. That, or she masturbated next to us with her eyes closed. What did she think of herself or Matt in this moment? I remember watching pornos where the girl would close her eyes as she was being fucked and keep them closed during the whole process as if to say, "I'm not here in this strange room, and there aren't cameras, this is just a person fucking me." I sometimes forgot that the three of us were in this strange game together, that she was prey or she was not.

I closed my eyes as well, and forgot I was trying to be a part of some young nuclear family, a girlfriend to a couple with a kid, a girl who lived in her mom's trailer and snorted her mom's Vicodin. I forgot that I was just a girl working at RadioShack who had slept with her manager, that I was just a girl, that I was me, that I was anything except for the thing Frankie named me, that I was anything else but Lilith.

TRANSCENDENTAL LOVE

FRANKIE AND I WERE watching the baby while Matt was at work. Patrick and his girlfriend Maya, whom I hadn't seen since we all went to the Satellite, came over with beer and ice cream. Patrick and Maya had a baby, too. We sat around and bullshitted on the couch and watched the two kids play with plastic toys sprawled out in the middle of the living room.

Patrick usually bought us liquor when he came over. He was twenty-one, and it seemed like he had a lot more connections than I did when it came to finding weed or harder recreational drugs. At the hotel, he had asked for my phone number when Maya wasn't looking. I gave it to him, hoping he would hook me up. I also hoped he would be a good source of information on Matt and Frankie's relationship, as if he might inadvertently show me cracks to exploit in order to get closer to one or both of them.

Patrick hadn't texted me much yet, but I liked having his number in my phone when neither Matt, Frankie, or Maya knew about it.

At Frankie's house, Maya revealed to me that her parents did not know Patrick was the father of their baby. She had told them the baby was from a one-night stand. I asked why. Maya waited until Patrick went outside to smoke a cigarette and then told me that they were first cousins.

I hadn't guessed that they looked so much alike because they were related. Maya had three sisters and a tight relationship with her mother, something I envied. Maya wanted Patrick to live with her. I wondered why they didn't just run away. I didn't understand that family was a thing that kept people rooted. It must have been hard to keep those kinds of secrets.

I watched both babies as they played, taking toys from one or the other, throwing things, sharing. If Maya and Patrick stayed in the city, the kids would grow up together like siblings.

I couldn't imagine staying in the Springs for my mom, who was the only real family I had. Maybe if I'd met someone and started a family. Even then, I wasn't sure if I could ever be a mother. I was an only child and selfish and inside of myself a lot, and I liked being that way. The way Jett spilled his food and then reached for Frankie, crying for someone to clean up his messes. The way he reached up when she walked by.

Jett was a thing that needed her. Jett was a thing that clung to her clothes and skin, clung to her hips, deeper than a tattoo. The way her body was shaped, her hips careened outward, the place where the child sat. He shook his plastic toys violently, threw them, broke things, tore paper. A chaotic animal. I used to think babies were fragile and weird and that you had to talk to them like they were something else, something dumber than you. They know when you think they're dumb or different, they pick that kind of stuff up. They unfold the way people do. It was too much, to take care of a thing like that.

Matt came home from work. Frankie and I sat on the living room floor cross-legged, Patrick and Maya on the couch. Jett was in Frankie's lap. I had a tiny basketball that squeaked. Jett squealed and tried to crawl toward me. He looked up as Daddy walked into the living room. I rolled the tiny basketball toward Jett, and as it stopped right in from him, he picked it up with his cherub fingers and stretched his arms out wide into a V, the muscles locking up so hard from excitement they shook. I laughed. I wanted to show Matt and Frankie that I could be useful, I could fit into their lives.

Matt stopped in the doorway. For a second, it felt like we were playing house—like Jett had two mothers and this father who worked. I wonder if in the past, people did live like this. Sometimes it felt tribal to be this way, as if we were a group of degenerates, isolated but entwined.

Jenny told me I was crazy to believe that I could ever be part of their family, some permanent fixture, the same way she said it was crazy to think Maya and Patrick would ever run away together.

I wanted to say she was wrong. For a time, being with the three of them was the only way I wanted to exist. I told Jenny that because I positioned myself as an expendable person, I never got jealous. I never allowed myself to feel jealous, to feel what it would be like to be number one.

I was an object in her eyes. I was a tool. Every time I heard the name Lilith, pieces of me slipped and gave way underneath her perception of me. I didn't need to prove I was better or more deserving because I knew I was expendable and let it be. Girl from the dirt.

At first.

It's inviting. It's inviting to a man who struggles with his spouse, latent loneliness, to a man who doesn't think long-term. A man who is obsessed with immediate satisfaction. Maybe I am projecting. The ultimate prize is someone who is unattached, who is not going to ask you to do menial tasks or subject you to their near-constant depression. It's inviting to spend time with someone who asks nothing of you but your presence, who does not ask you to invest anything other than your time. A girl who only wants your company, who is "down to fuck."

But it wasn't real. Which I guess we should have been used to, me and him.

THE WAY TO SURVIVE THE WORLD IS BY
MANIPULATING EVERYONE AROUND YOU

IT HAD BEEN ABOUT six months since we'd started "dating." I was at Matt and Frankie's house almost every night I wasn't working at Radioshack. And when I was, I came over after my shift. The relationship had grown from me as a sexual object to me as something more useful, multifaceted. I helped with dishes, cleaned or watched Jett if Frankie needed to shower. As they became more comfortable with me, they began to fight. Or maybe they had always fought this much, but they were no longer afraid to reveal their flaws in front of me.

Sometimes, their fights looked like harmless bickering, but soon their comments became more pointed and hurtful.

One night, I arrived at about eight, coming over after a shift. I hadn't eaten yet, but knowing their schedule, I assumed they'd either have eaten already or just be sitting down before putting the baby to bed. I put my hand on the cold knob to turn it, but I heard faint yelling from the other side of the door and decided to wait. I stilled every muscle in my body and slowed my breath as much as I could. It was a private moment, I thought; better for them to work things out before I came over. They were expecting me, but I figured they'd lost track of time.

I heard the deep bass of Matt's voice and then the rising screech of Frankie's. The yelling moved past the door, from one end of the apartment to the other. My heartbeat quickened every time. I wondered if one of them might come to the front door and swing it open unexpectedly, their angry faces seething at my spying. When I was young, I'd listen at my parents' bedroom door after they'd put me to bed, willing my ears to take in as much as I could.

Banging from the kitchen. I tried so hard to make out what Matt and Frankie were saying, wondered if they knew how loud they were being, if they cared that someone else could hear. How we act when we know we're being watched is so different. I stilled myself until my muscles ached, cupped my hands, and pressed my ear against the door.

"You don't have to repeat yourself, I heard you the first time."

"Then what are you doing?"

"Are you okay? Is there something wrong with you?"

"*Stop.* I've told you this time and time again—"

"Why is it such a big deal, are you hurt about it?"

The banging continued until I heard Frankie's voice rise into a guttural howl.

"Don't patronize me. I have to clean up your mess all the time, over and over again, I have to clean up after the child over and over again. Do not make this harder on me. You can take your shoes off or you can eat dinner outside."

"Jesus. You were fine earlier and I don't know what happened."

"*Fine,*" she said.

I heard footsteps toward the door and panicked. I jumped as quickly as I could to the side of the door, in between the apartment and the hedges, as it swung open violently.

Frankie's voice, now unmuffled, said, "Here's your dinner, bitch!" And then something ceramic broke against the front walk. She seemed unhinged and free, like she'd had to perform for so long. I could see Frankie's face contorted into anger. She looked like that a lot now: her brows knotted, the muscles in her body tense, her whole face in that new way, the stranger her. "If I had a fucking shotgun, I would have shot you by now!"

The door stayed open what seemed like a long time. I hoped she would close the door and this would all go away. I couldn't decide if showing up as if nothing had happened was a good idea, or if I should leave and go home for the night.

I had two paths. One was toward righteousness. If I went home and waited, I could come back when Matt was at work and comfort Frankie. We might sit at the kitchen table drinking coffee while I asked if she was okay, while I prodded, shared the experiences of my own tumultuous family, gradually worked her open. I would highlight the ways in which we were alike, conjecture that we were both women and thus somehow similar, facing a common enemy. She could find repose from her anger within me.

I imagined it in my head: us being *friends*. Being able to gain her trust. If I could comfort her in her time of need, she might be willing to let me in.

The other path was the one I was more familiar with. It was the path of sex. I could feel the manipulative part of myself light up like a highway at dusk. I felt sorry for Matt. I wanted to be the girl that was subdued for him instead of angry. I remember thinking how harsh it was for her to say that, *I would have shot you by now*, how violent it seemed, despite how physically violent Matt was during sex. I played the situation over and over in my head, the movement of the muffled voices, the door swinging open, the plate breaking against the concrete. And then how it was quiet for so long. Matt's voice said something low and inaudible. The door closed. My phone vibrated in my pocket as the door was clicking shut, and I almost died from the noise. It was a text from Patrick.

—*hey dude*

Real casual.

—*matt and frankie fighting*, I responded. *they always do this?*

I contemplated telling him where I was, hiding in the hedges. It felt comical. I worried it might make me look like a coward or some kind of stalker.

—*should i leave you think?*

I put my phone on silent and placed it in my lap, in case he texted back.

It had been silent for several minutes. I decided I should knock, to check in on them. I stood there for a few moments catching my breath, then heard what sounded like a scuffle and an angry scream. I opened the door right as it happened, just in time to see Matt holding her by the shoulders.

"I hate you!" she shouted, and then "*Stop*," from Matt.

The light was shining onto that long dark hair of hers, the halo of it around her head. Her amber eyes, I couldn't look straight into them. She stood there, Matt holding her, and they both looked at me. It was then I made my decision.

SELF-DECEIT IS NOT UNDEFILED WISDOM

THINGS CALMED DOWN OVER the next few days. I didn't ask questions about the fight, and neither of them talked to me about it. It was reminiscent of the fights I remembered my parents having, shouting about his drinking problem and how much money he spent on irresponsible things. Matt and Frankie simply moved on, as if nothing had happened.

The three of us lay together in bed. I woke up slightly as I heard Frankie stir, but I kept my body faced away from them. I was on the edge, facing the wall. Frankie was farthest from me. Matt lay between us.

I heard Frankie whisper, "Daddy, I'm horny."

He said, "It's three a.m. I have work in the morning."

She said, "I might have to watch a movie in the living room or something," whispering so the baby didn't wake up. Her whisper cloyed its way into my chest. My heart rate spiked with the thrill of voyeurism, like I was witnessing something I wasn't supposed to.

The weight of her body left the bed and I heard the soft pads of her feet move to the hallway. The milklight of early morning melted through the blinds in the bedroom. I stroked the new skin of the foxglove tattoo between my thighs, the scar rippling gently like silk.

Matt rolled over to me. His breath was hot and slept in, heavy and milky like the light. He pressed his lips against my neck, pushing harder with his mouth until his lips opened up beneath the weight.

I felt the hardness of his front teeth against my skin. He bit a little and said, "L."

I moved myself up against his body and made a noise like I was sleeping, a soft *mm* sound.

"I want to see the color of your blood again," he said in between a whisper and hum.

He said, "I really like you, Lilith."

His hands crept around my waist, the whole of my backside lying perfectly into the whole of his front side. My back curved against his chest, his stomach, my ass in his crotch, down to the warmth of his thighs against mine. I tried to get us to fit closer and he pulled me in tight. What it feels like to be held close to the ribs.

I mumbled a little. The riled-up beating of my heart went into my lungs and throat and ears, but I kept my eyes closed. I wouldn't let my voice betray me. When I responded, I wanted him to know I was aware of what he was doing and that I was okay with it, as if this slight betrayal wasn't anything unusual at all. I whispered back, "I really like you too, Matt."

His body pressed harder, fitting his knees into the crook of my own.

"No, girl," he whispered. "I don't think you understand."

I turned my head around to look at him. He wasn't smiling, not even smirking. He wasn't staring at my third-eye spot. He was staring directly into my eyes. I was close enough that I could see the way his eyes moved back and forth between my right eye and left, reading my face for a response. His tenderness was both jarring and intoxicating, and felt like a glimpse into the private life he had built with Frankie. I envied it desperately even as I had his full attention, a deep sucking desire to hold his words inside of me—words that Frankie would never know—and tongue them gently in the soft tissues of my gut as if those words, his tenderness, might one day disappear. Matt had told me there were nine tenets in Satanism and that the first of these was indulgence, the fifth one being vengeance. Maybe that holy fear was letting go of self-judgment, of accepting what was an innate truth about human behavior, that we are just animal, nothing more. In all of us, there is light and there is dark. We feed that dark part of ourselves through daily actions, and a syntax builds to create the person you become.

I figured it would be the closest to inside each other we'd ever get. The real inside, not vagina inside. The inside with all the guts and glory, where the fear and love lives. There's something about closing another person out that hardens what you have. We lay there embryonic. You and me against your girlfriend. You and me against the mother of your child.

That's why Frankie named me Lilith. She saw me for who I was, the dark and rotten feminine.

I was the bad woman.

It was predictable.

Perhaps because it was much easier than being good.

In their bed, Matt and I alone, I turned all the way around to face him, my knees between his. I grabbed his hands and placed them on my ribs, wanted to feel him squeeze so I couldn't breathe. I moved back and forth with my hips slightly and he moved a hand to my mouth. I tilted my chin down and sucked on the tip of his finger.

"You're the devil," I said.

"The devil isn't real," Matt said. "Black magic and all of that, it's not real."

The dawn was creeping in, a soft shade of pastel blue that washed across Matt's pale skin.

"What do you mean, like animal sacrifices and shit?"

"Well, yeah," he said. "Satanism isn't really about that. It's about the dark shit, the untouched parts of your mind."

"The places where the light don't touch," I said.

"It's experiencing for yourself the bad things you've done to others."

Some erotic feeling in me stirred and then flowered. I felt powerful, predatory and scared.

That's what drew me into Matt's embrace: acceptance of the dark part of myself, the rejection of the light. The pale blue surrounded us, our bodies an illuminated text in the milk light bed. We were there, alone. This is what it would be like to be just us.

The toilet flushed from the hallway and I remembered Frankie. Matt took his hand back. The baby stirred in his crib. I turned away and pretended to be asleep.

The day after, I showed up to Jenny's house with a bottle of vodka and pills in my backpack. I ran from my car to her front door and knocked frantically.

Jenny's neighborhood was in a place I wouldn't walk around alone at night, next to the oldest Wal-Mart in Colorado Springs. She opened the creaking screen door and let me in.

"I have something to tell you," I blurted out breathlessly.

"What's going on?"

I took the crumpled bag of liquor out of my backpack and handed it to her. We moved into the dimly lit kitchen of her house, the soft light making her look sweet and inviting. Her mom was working, I suspected, and her dad asleep. We didn't have to go downstairs just yet.

"I'll tell you," I said, "but first, drinks."

Jenny poured vodka into two coffee mugs. I thought about the holy fear Matt described. Did he live with it or was he free? Did he accept his dark parts wholly and unrestrained, and could I? With clothes on, he was so calm. Slow, thoughtful in his actions. Restrained. He had a sense of patience with Frankie and his kid. Underneath was something else. I considered his potential capacity to inflict emotional or physical damage on me. When he had pulled me closer to him, it felt so good I wasn't sure if I cared about the consequences.

"Jenny, I'm obsessed with him. And Frankie is so crazy I don't know how to deal with it."

She grabbed a plastic bottle of Cherry Coke from the fridge and untwisted the top.

"Matt is easy to obsess over," she said. "He just has that way about him. But he and Frankie have been on and off since freshman year of high school." She poured soda into each of the cups and then handed me one. "That won't end easily."

Something in me was changing, even then in the kitchen with Jenny. A part of me was opening up, and while I could see the end of the road and new that it would lead to pain, instead of retreating, I wanted to walk directly into it. Pain is closer to love than indifference, right? I wanted to walk directly into it.

"On and off isn't good for relationships," I said. "They'll never last."

"How long are you willing to wait?"

I took a sip from the thick lip of the mug and set my cup back down on the counter, remembering the pills. I pulled two tabs of Percocet from me bag. She shook her head at me.

"We have to do that downstairs," she said.

"It just seemed so intense, you know? Like a forever feeling," I said. "I could fuck him forever."

She leaned her elbow against the linoleum counter. Her blunt bangs were a little long and they fell in her face, dark roots growing from her scalp.

"So? I could fuck *you* forever," she said. She took another sip of her drink. I loved this, whatever we were doing. She leaned in close and pressed her lips against mine, still wet from the drink. It felt so easy with her. I thumbed the pills in my palm as she kissed me.

"Look," she said. "I think you should follow your heart if it feels right. But I don't know what Frankie would do. In high school, she fought girls over Matt. Like, beat the shit out of them."

I pouted my lips and imagined Matt's presence in my body. "But I like him."

"I know, sweet cheeks." She tugged on my sweater and led me downstairs.

THE OTHER WAY TO SURVIVE THE WORLD
IS TO GO TO RAVES

IT WAS THE END of winter, and we were dancing in the middle of the night at a warehouse off Marksheffel Road. I had persuaded Sam and Jenny to come out with me. We'd taken ecstasy and the sweat sparkled on our faces against the backdrop of flashing lights. In the center of the dance floor, people packed in shoulder to shoulder and Rabbit in the Moon played ethereal lava music with a thunderous house beat. Each body in the room swayed together like a single organism. The subwoofer was a heartbeat threading through the crowd. The warehouse was wet and musky and the smells of our bodies mixed and pulsed.

What's so beautiful about ecstasy is the start of it. There's a swollen feeling that slowly flickers into your chest and then burns through the rest of your body. It feels like doing a new drug all of the time, like an extended, slow-release orgasm.

Matt, Frankie, and Jenny went to sit in some alcove with pillows and string lights, leaving Sam and me alone on the dance floor. I wished it was Matt who had stayed behind, but I took the chance to kiss Sam on his neck and then gently on the lips while we danced. Still, I didn't want to miss out on anything Matt was doing. I led Sam with me to the alcove, where we found the three of them sitting with a new guy wearing a Dr. Seuss hat and a flashing necklace. He had dark hair and a really big smile. The new guy, who called himself Tasty, sat between Jenny and Frankie. He pulled out a small dark vial and asked us all if we were rolling. My lips curled up toward my cheeks and into the clouds.

My eyes widened when he poured whatever was into the vial onto a house key, moony in his shining hands.

"It's K," he said.

Matt took the first hit. Tasty held the key the whole time even though his hands were shaky. He'd put it right under someone's nose and the powder would disappear like it never existed.

Tasty got to me next. It was intimate. The heat and skin of his hand gently scraped my cheek as he put the key under my nose. I closed the other nostril just like everyone else and sniffed until the powder was gone. Everything smelled like dish detergent for a second before the world got soft and spongy and sweet. I felt like a bag of marshmallows, plastic and all, expanding and melting inside of a safe, hot microwave. Sam liked me and Jenny liked me and Matt was telling everyone I was his girlfriend's girlfriend. In that moment Everyone Loved Me and I didn't want it to change.

I leaned into Frankie and felt closer to her than ever before.

"I have to tell you something," I said. Our hands touched and instinctively each of our fingers began to writhe in sensation, dumping endorphins into our bodies.

"You can tell me anything, Lilith." She smiled at me as though someone was teasing her.

"When I heard you guys fighting, I wanted to come in and rescue you." I don't know what motivated me to say this. The sentiment was hollow, but once I started, I couldn't stop. "I just really care about you, I want us to be friends and more than friends."

She gasped and then pulled me close. "We *are* more than friends," she said. She began to laugh and stroke my hair. I moved my hand to her neck and her skin was so soft. I knew the entire moment was contrived but I didn't care, and I continued to tell her embarrassing things about how I longed for her companionship. She kissed me and I felt like a door had been unlocked somehow, but I knew it wouldn't carry through to morning.

My phone flashed—a text from Patrick. I ignored it. He had been texting me more every day. I had been sending smiley faces after each text and was always nice. But right now I didn't need him. I didn't need to work an angle because everything felt so perfect.

Tasty asked me if I'd ever had a Seabreeze before. I said no. He moved us so that we were sitting cross-legged and facing each other and I smiled. He put a Vicks inhaler in his mouth and started rubbing my face in a really nice way.

"You can't kiss me, okay?" he said. I nodded as he massaged the fatty part of my cheeks. He started blowing air from his mouth, metabolized by the inhaler. I closed my eyes against the astringent feeling and imagined myself on some beach, a place I'd never been. Suddenly, it felt like there were many hands massaging me, rubbing my shoulders and arms, releasing tension. Then someone, I think Tasty, reached out of the dark and pried my eyelids open, breathing hard into each eye. A disembodied voice that sounded like his told me to breathe in deeply, and when I did, the ocean feeling filled my mouth and nose, burning like a cold fire. When I touched my face, my eyes were leaking hot liquid and the ocean feeling spread across my cheeks. I fell back into someone's arms and disappeared into myself.

I heard Frankie's voice against my ear, but I couldn't see anything. She placed her hand on my hand and then pulled me up out of my seat and into what felt like a whole new world. Walking was floating. We moved together the way two wind currents might gently meet on a calm summer day.

It felt like a different Frankie. Our mouths fell into each other as if I was with Jenny. How I wanted things to be, easy. How it was a secret but it was our secret.

My vision came back slowly and the intense ocean feeling faded. We did another bump of K. The rising feeling in my chest stopped just before the climax, rode out slow. Back in the alcove of pillows and string lights, I made out with Matt, moving my mouth and tongue around the whole cosmic world. Frankie was on the dance floor, moving in between Jenny and Sam.

Everything was right and in tune with what needed to happen. In the heavy music, Matt yell-whispered words I couldn't hear.

"What?" I shouted.

Matt moved his body into my body and put his mouth right at my ear. This muffled, blown-out speaker sound came out of his mouth.

"I HAVE REALLY STRONG FEELINGS FOR YOU."

Matt moved away from my face, his eyes holding this innocent, childish look. In the mix of UV and dark and flashing lights, I felt dizzy. The lights flashed white; he put his hand on my waist and moved his fingers up the hem of my shirt. The bridge piercing between his eyes reflected every flash and my cloud-covered high zoomed in on the perfect intensity of his lips. He gripped the side of me, began to massage my skin, and the ocean feeling came back. The lights flashed purple, the music beat against me, the sweat on his chest was coming through his shirt. I stared at the tattoos on his upper arms, his chest, his eyes, his lips. The lights flashed a pale blue. I fell into him and placed my lips against his and we kissed and it was warm and the boundary dissolved between us until in the music there were just the two of us and no one else. Then the adrenaline rush, water hitting air and wet sand, waves cresting. It moved through my body, from the place where I bit my lip down to my core.

The music reverberated against the walls like a hymn through a large, empty church. I pulled away from him, feeling drunk, like I was inside a very humid cloud. My vision bludgeoned from his touch. He grabbed my wrist and pulled me closer, said he wanted to *make love to me*, not just animal-fuck. I put my hands together in prayer and he kept his hands wrapped around my wrists. I wanted his hands to squeeze tighter, to crush the bones into a single mass.

In the deep house beat with all the lights flashing, I kept my eyes closed and my hands in prayer and thought *Daddy*.

"I want to get closer to you," he said. "Want to know you. Want to run away." Matt pressed his body against mine through the heavy fog that felt so good. He said the words again, one by one, into my mouth.

"We could run away together, you know?" he said. "A place with evergreens growing, a place we can sleep in every Sunday morning. I'll put you through college, whatever you want. Take me with you there."

There were bruises on my body from the way we'd all been fucking. I pulled my hands out of prayer. "I want that too," I said, chewing my tongue. "I want to feel like you own me, like you have all of me." He looked so good in this moment with his heart beating sweat out of his chest and his pouty lips and because he was a father, whatever that reason was. Because I could hear the way Frankie called him *Daddy*, and I wanted to possess those moments the way she seemed to possess them so effortlessly.

The next morning I had another text from Patrick.

—*whats up whatcha doing?*

—*not much, headed back to springs*, I wrote back.

—*have u ever seen frankie threaten m?* I added.

I folded my phone over and over in my lap, seated next to Jenny on the drive back from the rave. The sun painted the trailer park all of the beautiful pastel colors of dawn. At home, I drank water hungrily and searched my room for candy or some lollipop to satiate my grinding teeth. Goa seemed like an appropriate soundtrack for my comedown, so I turned on a playlist and lay in bed to think about Matt and our moment, the way his fingers feathered over my skin in the flashing lights, his mouth hot in my ear and the words repeating over and over again.

I want to get closer to you.
I want to get closer to you.
I want to get closer to you.

Frankie was nowhere to be found. We were alone, my hands on his arms. I was lost in the visceral snap of hot air and the electric lights.

I want to get closer to you.

I was still pretty high. The skinfeeling of Matt's body burned against me, a shadow echo of the night. I felt like his skin was still in my hands and mouth. Each minute of the comedown, the feeling became sand against my palms, my body became beach water, wet, lapped against the shores of his disintegrated body. The vignettes moved through my body in lulled pulses until I could no longer take it. I chewed what remained of the lollipop, chewed through the stick, and dug into my closet looking for art supplies, throwing boxes of torn-up magazines, old glue sticks, and paints onto the floor.

I settled on a small piece of cottonwood I collected from a car accident I got into once. I hit this log in the road while driving to work, thinking that it would go right in between my tires. I misjudged. The wood swung right up into my wheel well and popped up the driver's side of the car. The tire was blown. I was right near work, so I stopped on the side of the road and called Sam to tell him I'd be late.

In five minutes, he had pulled up in his '99 Camaro. It was cold and overcast and we could see our breath. I did not ask who was watching the store while he was there, jacking the car up. He tried pulling the lug nuts off with his bare hands and scraped his knuckles on the asphalt.

"You don't have to do that," I said. The smell of burning tires rushed by on the asphalt. The way cold air makes things louder, sound travels faster. The way cold air sharpens the way everything feels.

Sam, in his fleece jacket, lanyard hanging out of his pocket.

"Shut up," he said.

Sam didn't see it, but I walked into the road to retrieve the piece of wood. Some kind of talisman for a time when someone cared for me. The way love is a power. The way it's uneven, it can be abused. Here was somebody doing something nice for me in a way that no one else had before. Me and that daddy-shaped hole. His breath hit the air, making little clouds as he breathed.

Eventually he got the tire off and the donut on the car. I made it to work and back home that night

The Goa was still playing in my room and the drugs were wearing off. If I rubbed my skin or myself the right way, I still got little electric tingles through my body. If I let myself focus on the part of Matt I loved the most, his pouty lips, the cupids bow, I could close my eyes and let it flower into his face, face soaked into soft neck and neck into body. Hands into hair. I touched my hips, felt my pelvic bones and the raised scar tissue of the tattoo on my belly and thigh. The new skin, I felt my hand touch it, and I grabbed, tried to grab the way Matt would, the way he would sink his nails in and almost rip.

I pulled out my phone and composed a text message in the hopes of securing his attention.

—*i fucking want you*

Looking at the words on the screen, they seemed too aggressive. I deleted them and tried for something else.

—*what could you possibly be doing other than thinking about me*

That still wasn't right.

—*are you thinking about me?*

Too needy.

—*what are you doing?*

Which didn't get to the heart of what I wanted, which was:

—*can't you just talk to me instead of be with her*

I deleted that too, and then,

—*does she let you choke her*

I watched the blinker blinking text and then deleted it.

I put my phone away, lay down, and finally slept.

HURT ME IF YOU WANT TO HURT ME

HOW DOES AN OBSESSION grow? Slowly, like a mold? The spores settle unseen and then blooms form, devouring any open brainscape. The genitals become infected quickly. I'm not sure how this process works exactly. A feedback loop. Mycelium reaches out, ridge by beating ridge, a thought, a heart rate rises, a feeling like sex or love, then another thought. Each pulse a quickening like river beneath the soil.

I could feel Matt there in my head, a bloom connecting to other toxic parts of me. I woke up manic. The pulsing thoughts kept pushing my muscles toward action, so I had to keep moving my hands, grabbed the piece of cottonwood and broke it into pieces. I carved into the wood with a knife. It felt so good to tense my fingers around this tiny object, to feel the wood rub against the ditches of my hands, the give of each chip or shaving. I held it in my hands, nicks and cuts on my knuckles, my muscles so tense they went numb. I tried to make a heart. Eventually I had something in the shape of a deformed egg. There was blood on my fingers and stuck to the wood. It seemed appropriate, blood on a misshapen heart. That I had failed to bring my vision to fruition made it an appropriate symbol of my struggle with Matt. That I had recycled a talisman from someone else also seemed accurate, like something I would do.

I looked for sandpaper in my closet to smooth out the rough edges. There were divots in the wood that I couldn't work into. The blood on my hands, I rubbed it into the cottonwood. I figured I could paint over it, and my blood was a good gift to give Matt.

My phone vibrated. It was Patrick.

—*sometimes, frances does get violent, idk. its kinda crazy.*

—*idgi. why?*

—*shes just a control freak. you know? she gets angry when she can't have her way.*

Matt started coming by during my breaks at work. He called during his lunch breaks to ask if I was working the evening shift, and I usually was. I saw him walking up before he got into the store. The sky was this blue-gray color, the sun setting. You never see it set on the horizon here. It sets over the mountains—Pikes Peak, specifically, the closest mountain to the city. Everyone moves here because they think it's beautiful, but it's not. It's not romantic, because the city is full of decrepit buildings that crowd the view. Dozens of car-sale complexes sit in the foothills, and behind that, the houses of rich people who never have to drive into the potholed neighborhoods below.

Matt had his hands in his hoodie pockets and followed his feet with his eyes. We locked stares through the glass when he got to the door. I finished ringing up the customer I had and turned to look at Jenny at the other register, her bangs in her face, ringing up video games and smiling at customers. Without missing a beat, she nodded at me.

"Go," she said. "I'll cover you."

I stopped in the backroom to quickly check my phone.

—*what are you doing tonight?*

Another text from Patrick.

—*can't talk now, later sweet thing* I texted back. I had begun using pet names to tempt him into opening up to me, to gather intel.

Outside in the cold, I shivered in my polo and khakis even though the sun was shining. A sudden cold snap had hit. We were just around the corner of the building, out of sight. Matt stood an arm's length away from me and I leaned against the concrete of the building, resting my head against the wall.

"I love coming to see you," Matt said.

I moved closer to him. I wanted to feel the bass of his voice reverberate through his chest when he said the words "love" and "you."

"I want to see you alone," I said. "Like, more often, not just this."

I knew I was crossing a line. It was something I felt I shouldn't demand, as the other woman. As a woman trying to get something from him. He had to want to give things to me.

"We will," he said. "I'm trying to find time."

I asked myself if he really loved Frankie. If maybe he wanted me because I treated him more sweetly. I asked nothing of him. When you don't live with someone, you don't get to see their imperfect facets. The mean side of them. The impatient, ungrateful side. Those things are revealed later, often when it's too late. It was easy to see why he might want me, why I might be an uncomplicated addition to his life. I was molding myself to some image, trying to be better than what he already had. In these limited moments, he was able to project what he wanted onto me. I was happy to let him have whatever idea of me he wanted. Jealousy came from the fear of being replaced. I was The Replacer.

"It's just harder now to control my feelings," I told him, an unusual admission of truth. I had thought the truth would set me free, but it had not. I felt more trapped than before. The brainbloom of my obsession with him took up too much space in my head. I had become attached, and there was nothing I could do to go back.

I did not know what I expected him to say. I hooked my finger into his belt loop, tugged him a little closer to me. I bit my bottom lip and looked up at him. It was like a math equation, the way to charm him.

"Don't you want me?" I asked.

I wanted to see what kind of sway I had over him. Our bodies near each other. In my head, we could be falling for each other and that meant I was winning. I had a feeling he would leave Frankie. He seemed to want to escape her. I wanted to escape the city. I saw no reason why we couldn't run away together. We could move away from this town, away from Frankie, away from Sam, from the jobs we had and the blight of Colorado Springs and my mom's trailer. A place of our own, our own wraparound velvet couch in some garden-level apartment. I even imagined taking the baby. We would be a family. Someday, he and I would share that one-bedroom apartment with Jett in the crib.

Someday I'd be calling Matt *Daddy* and he'd answer only to me.

"I do, I want you," he said, his pouty mouth soft and relaxed. "I just need some time."

A few weeks had passed since the rave. His hair had grown longer, enough to run my fingers through it.

I put my hand inside my pocket and fished out the wooden egg-heart. I felt it with its divots and jagged edges and clenched my fingers around it, fitting the whole of it into the palm of my hand. I clutched Matt's own hand and spread his fingers open, watched his eyes as he looked down at what I was doing. I placed it into his palm and pushed each finger down until his hand made a fist around it. It felt like I was always waiting for him to put his hands on my neck. There was nothing I didn't want to give him. I wanted him to hurt me if he wanted to hurt me. I wanted to explore the limits of my own pain, to push my psychological limits. I'd never been scared of the power of men before him. When he said he needed time, I resolved to give it to him.

It was the first time I was truly vulnerable with someone else. It was the first time I was so wild in my lust that I lost myself, let myself fall in love without worrying about the consequences. I just wanted to be vulnerable, to let the restrictions go and let someone else control me, to be ripped open raw. Dick-drunk fucked into love.

"I want you to know every part of me," I said. I chewed on my tongue and wondered if it would always feel this way, illegal. Matt looked down at the heart in his hands and took a deep breath in.

"I think I'm falling in love with you, Lilith," he said.

Matt's shadow shielded the setting sun. The way he was standing, a halo of light hovered just behind his head. The closest we could be was fucking when Frankie was watching, her hands on my thighs. We had never been alone long enough to have sex just the two of us. I knew I was romanticizing the longing too much, but I wanted the pain. My heart was beating too hard. I wanted it to be wrong. Our moments, we'd keep them. I thought it would win him over, that it was what he wanted. That's what I thought in that moment, like I was in a fucking romance novel, saying stupid shit like *I want you to know every part of me.*

I reasoned with myself by attempting to lie. I told myself it wasn't my attraction to him that was making me feel this way, but that I was addicted to doing the wrong things. Breaking the rules felt wrong at first, but it was exciting. It raised the stakes. I liked to do drugs, so it was only natural I would also like to do other bad things. Sleeping with Sam, my boss. Hiding the relationship with this couple from Sam and my mom and everybody. Stealing my mother's drugs. Sleeping with Jenny, who was supposed to be a friend. Breaking the rules by being emotional with Frankie, and then going behind her back with Matt. The last and final rule: don't fall in love with a taken man. A man who is a father, who is committed not just through lust but through his own blood.

Yes. It had to be that. I was just a rule-breaker. Girl from dirt, not from rib. I looked at Matt, not into his eyes. I looked at his third-eye spot. Matt said it again: "I think I'm falling in love with you."

I didn't say it back.

THE SATANIC BIBLE SAYS MAN IS
JUST ANOTHER ANIMAL

I'M PRETTY SURE THE meaning of life is about sex. Otherwise, why do we suffer so much for it? Why do guys get jobs they hate? Why do men marry women they don't like? Why do girls do the stupid shit they do? Why do they all seem so fucking unhappy? This whole game is just a giant trick to get us to fuck each other and make more ugly people until the Earth burns. *Solve et coagula.* People die, they become dirt, people are born, they suffer, they fuck, give birth, die, dirt. Over and over again. Everything in between is us running away from it. Even if you never make babies, there's some bullshit in your blood that just pushes you to fuck people. The sooner we all accept that, the easier our lives will be.

When I talked to Jenny, it wasn't because I loved her. That is in-between shit. That is crazy-making. It is the shit that makes me drink, probably, my daddy-shaped hole. Really, I just couldn't stop thinking about the way her body felt against mine.

Like with Patrick. Why was I naïve enough to think he just wanted to be friends?

Maybe I wasn't that naïve.

Attention feels so good. Surely some god made me like this. Otherwise, why the fuck was I chasing it so hard?

When I gave Patrick my number, what I wanted was information about Matt and Frankie. I knew that some biological undercurrent would pull him toward me. He was in his early twenties. I was nineteen.

I also knew about the situation with his cousin. I texted him about it because I was too much of a coward to ask in person. *are you going to be with her forever, why don't you just move away from your family and get married?*

It seemed as though he wasn't very happy with her. Maybe it wasn't true love after all. That was disappointing. I had hoped it was true love, that something like that could exist. Instead, it was just sex. Like everything else.

This was confirmed when Patrick texted me the very same words Matt whispered against my ear. It did not have nearly the same effect.

—*i really like you*, said the message.

I tried so hard to get Sam's attention and he was so fucking stingy with it. He was on and off ignoring me. And here was Matt, and his friend Patrick—these two men whose lives I just showed up in and they were perfectly willing to give me all of the attention I wanted. I wondered if this was how Frankie felt, being in control all the time.

They were so willing to spurn their girlfriends. They did this, put their relationships at risk, when they both had *children*, that supposed ultimate proof of true love. I felt so confident and sure of my place, like I lived on a pedestal. I felt like a goddess, a wild demon woman. I felt like Lilith.

I was already committed to this thing with Matt, had already decided I would use any means to get between him and Frankie. I wanted to let go of the holy fear, the Puritanism. I wanted to serve Matt for myself and for him and not for anyone else.

On my lunch break, I was walking to the grocery store when I saw the brake lights of a familiar slate gray Chevy Malibu pull up to the entrance. A short brunette popped out of the car and ran into the store. I realized it was Frankie. Before the car could pull away, I ran up to it and peeped through the driver-side window.

It'd been about a week since I'd seen the two of them together, three days since I saw Matt alone. His elbow rested over the lip of the car door and he was wearing this Dickies work shirt with a gray crew neck underneath. God bless a man in Dickies.

"Well, howdy, stranger," I said.

I glanced at Jett in the backseat and then back at Matt. He bit his lip and said *mm*, this short-burst moan before he opened his mouth.

"Hi, girl," he said. "What are you doin'?"

"On break," I said. I learned over into the car and licked my teeth. Cars behind him started to pile up in line.

"Shit—" he said real long, broke it into two syllables like *sheee-yet*. "Get in."

I looked at the entrance and didn't see Frankie. Matt's glance followed mine and he winked.

"Come on," he goaded. "She'll be waiting for me in the store."

I loved the inside of his car. Leather seats, fancy blue lights everywhere. A good car meant a man with money, which really meant a man who was attractive was a man wasting his money on stupid shit. He pulled into a nearby parking spot and looked at me like I was supposed to know what to do next. I got on my knees in the seat and leaned over the armrest, smiling, moving my ass. Matt grabbed my face in his hands and pulled my mouth into his.

"Aren't you scared," I mouthed into his mouth.

"Shit, yeah," he said. Our mouths together, like darkness touching itself. He kissed me hard, quick, as if to make up for our short amount of time.

"I can't stop thinking about you," I mouthed to him again. I pulled my face away from his pouty lips. Even with the windows down, it was hot in the car. His hands moved to my body, grabbed my waist, my breasts. I looked over at the baby in the backseat.

That night, I lay down on my dirty carpet texting Jenny about my interactions with Matt and how fucked up it was he wasn't leaving Frankie yet.

—*i don't understand what's taking him so long*

Jenny shot back,

—*i told u tho*

I called their house with a blocked number in case Frankie answered, so I could hang up. I stared at my body as the phone rang, in a full-length mirror placed sideways. Watched my body writhe amongst the trash on my floor in red lingerie. I tried to see myself as Matt might see me underneath him.

"Hello?" It was Matt. The phone always took the bass out of his voice, but he sounded so close to me on the receiver.

"Hi, Daddy," I said. I had wanted to say it to him for so long, but the word sounded foreign in my mouth and I immediately regretted it. My body thrashed with the burn of a mistake. "I just wanted to hear you," I said. I felt embarrassed, and touched the red lingerie all over my body. "I'm not wearing much."

"Hm, really?" I could hear him speaking with that smirk he had.

Whatever was happening inside my body, these feelings, meant the love could last. Something told me he loved me, too. There was a pause. I imagined him taking a tube of Chapstick out of his pocket and applying it to his lips, the Cupid's bow glowing like a diamond.

"Tell me what you're wearing," I cloyed.

"I can't," he said. I could hear Jett crying in the background, Frankie's voice saying something.

"It's Patrick," he said to her. And then, "Look man, I gotta go. Dinner with the lady."

He hung up.

DAUGHTER OF SWORDS

I CAME OVER TO Jenny's with a bottle of vodka, asking her advice.

"You need some kind of power to help you with your shit," she said. I thought about the billboard on Chelton Road. Every time you drove east, there'd be this big sign that said PORN in big block letters on it, which an image of a white man's hands bound in the same thorny wire that crowned our lord and savior's head.

"Jesus?" I asked.

"Fuck no," she said.

Jenny flipped the tarot cards over one by one. The backs were blue with white flowers. She arranged them in the shape of a cross, and then added a pillar of four cards.

We sat in the basement amid a dozen lit candles. I poured vodka into my usual coffee mug. We were hunched, knees up to our chests, sitting on the floor with the cards laid out between us. I played a game. She'd flip a card over and I'd take a drink.

The card in the middle of the cross was a barn owl, like the one tattooed on my stomach. In the card, her wings were splayed wide and there was a sword in her clawed feet. Jenny called this card the Daughter of Swords.

"This woman is too rational," she said, pointing to the card. It didn't sound like she was talking about me. "The Daughter of Swords thinks too much, she cuts away any emotion in her life. She's afraid to let her feelings control her."

"But all I do is chase my feelings," I said.

"Maybe what you are doing is running from the real ones," she said.

Jenny delicately touched each card before flipping it over. I felt ashamed and jealous that she could know so much about me when I didn't understand why I was doing what I did at all.

On top of the Daughter of Swords was a card with an image of the Baphomet, the same one I saw on the Satanic Bible. In the card, the Baphomet's hands were pointed in the same way—as above, so below, *solve et coagula*.

"This card is about your own bondage," Jenny said. "You're letting yourself get trapped in a place you don't need to be trapped."

"Are you sure?" I looked at the image of the card, the way it covered the Daughter of Swords. The Devil, was he smothering me? Or was it a sign that Matt and I would be together?

The light of the candles moved shadows across Jenny's face, her bangs in her eyes. She looked concerned. She pointed to a picture of three people holding three cups, but the card was upside down, all the shit spilling out of the cards.

"This card says there's a third person involved," she said.

"No shit," I said. "Frankie?"

Jenny picked the card up and stared intently. She took a sip of her own drink and scanned the rest of the reading.

"I don't know," she said. "Not sure."

I never told Matt or Frankie that Patrick had asked me out. There were already too many complicated things going on. I didn't want anything to change just yet. Whenever I saw him and they were around, I'd pretended nothing happened, and he did the same.

Jenny moved her hand across a card at the top of the pillar. Her fingers stopped at an image of the Tower of Babel. A crown on top of the tower was being struck by lightning.

"This is the final outcome," she said. "Whoever that third person is, it's not a good idea to keep pursuing this thing with Matt."

I took another drink. Fire billowed out of the windows of the tower. Two people were falling to their deaths. One person in the card seemed to stare at me, their hands up in surrender, accepting their fate.

I woke up that morning in Jenny's bed to six missed phone calls. My mouth had that candy vomit hangover taste.

"Fuck," I said. 11:34 a.m. "Fuuuuuuuck."

I was late to work.

Jenny stirred, wiping the sleep from her eyes, her hair poking up in cute ways. I wished I could look as good as her in the morning.

"What's up?" she said.

"Gotta fucking go," I said. I slid out of bed and threw on a dirty pair of jeans. "Mind if I borrow a work shirt?"

She shook her head and pointed to her laundry hamper. I rummaged through and pulled out a black polo, a little old-smelling. I slid it over my head anyway, too impatient to throw on a bra first.

As I ran up the stairs, I checked the missed calls.

Frances

Frances

Frances

Frances

Frances

Frances

I hopped in my car and stuck the key in the ignition. The air was crisp but warming up a little. I called Frankie back, but no one answered. I didn't leave a voicemail.

•

The store was busy when I showed up. I got through the first four hours of my shift without stopping, keeping my head down, hoping Sam wouldn't say anything. I kept checking my phone for Frankie's call, but no one called me back. Around four, I saw Matt walk up to the store through the glass. He pulled the door open, hands in his hoodie pockets, looking down at his boots. From behind the counter, Sam said, "Can I help you?"

"I got it," I said, walking over. "What's up?"

It'd been at least two weeks since I'd seen him at the grocery store and a week since we'd last talked. My body burned at the sight of him, and my hands shook, though lately they were always shaking. I spent so much time waiting to hear from him that the lack of him made me crazy. He was the one with all the control, the one with the secret to keep. When I looked in his eyes, I saw something different this time, a kind of sadness, I guess. Some guilt. A strange kind of anger. He didn't put his hand out or on me like we knew each other.

"What's wrong?" I said. I put down the games I had been organizing.

Matt shook his head, this tiny little shake, and looked down. Sam stood at the counter and looked at Matt with one eyebrow raised.

"I'm gonna take my fifteen," I said. "Be back in a sec."

I led Matt outside and around the corner, just to the point where Sam couldn't see anymore. The sun was setting over the mountains. We were in the same spot we stood when he first told me he loved me. It made it all a little romantic. But Matt wasn't feeling romantic. He looked tense, like somebody had died.

"What the hell is going on?" I asked, impatient. My stomach turned and I felt a little nauseous.

Matt leaned against the wall and didn't say anything. He pulled out a cigarette, his hand cupping as he lit. He let it go, handed it to me, and pulled out another one.

"Frankie's breaking up with you," he said.

"Just Frankie?" I said. I almost laughed at that. "Like, for both of you?"

He nodded his head, eyes closed, like he couldn't look at me when he said it.

"Patrick was missing last night, you know," he said.

"The fuck?" I said. "Missing? Where was he?"

"Look, I'm not good at this shit," he said. "I know I've been lying to Frankie and all, but you're just lying to everybody. You lie to your boss, about your boss, you lie to Jenny, and now you're lying to *me*."

He put the cigarette to his mouth again and sucked in.

"You're lying to yourself, Lilith."

All the ways that he fucked me, the hard way, the honest way. An empty hunger rose in my body.

"You're perverse," he said. "You know? I should have known better."

"Better than *what*?"

"The messages. All over Patrick's phone!" he said. "You were talking to him this whole time? Maya came over and said you guys have been flirting for weeks. Do you just fuck anybody?"

"I have no idea what you're talking about," I said. I tensed the muscles in my throat. "I was with Jenny last night."

Everything was failing. My constant attempt to get us together *and* alone, trying to figure out our great escape, to figure out when he would leave Frankie behind so we could run away together, the way I had suggested for Patrick and Maya. Because that was a love full of bliss, with all their crazy cousin-fucking, transcendental love, the lies, hiding, and of course, the ultimate manifestation of their love, the baby. Their illegal Lilith fucking love.

Nothing was real.

"Sure," Matt said. "Sure, Lilith. Fucking Jenny too, I guess. Do you ever tell *yourself* the truth?"

I hadn't told him about Jenny yet, but I didn't think that he would care as much as he did. A hot buzz of embarrassment washed over my face. He cared, and that was exciting. To be possessed in some way. And now he was breaking up with me? Not him, but Frankie. And she sent him to do it? After all the time I spent getting him to sneak around, working up to being together, his fucking promises. The chance had come and instead he was breaking up with me. *That* was perverse.

The six missed calls made sense now. Frankie was the decision-maker. It had to be her. He was just doing her bidding, letting her control him.

With that, he stormed off. I ran after him until I got to the door of RadioShack.

"Matt!" I yelled. "Please don't leave!"

"Come get your shit later," he shouted back. I watched him walk to his Malibu, hands in his pockets, head down.

Everything I've heard about the night before they broke up with me is heresay. Bits and pieces from Jenny, from friends of friends.

What I heard was Maya stormed over to Matt and Frankie's. Frankie was her closest friend, the only other mom she knew. Frankie was also the only person Maya talked to about her relationship with Patrick.

This is how I picture it: Maya is there in the dining room. It is the same dining room I sat down in the first night I met Matt and Frankie, magazines and salt crumbs all over the table, high chair against the wall. The light is the same yellow light you always get when the sun sets, when it leaks through the blinds and shows how the dust has settled on every surface, how nothing is how it seems in the dark. Matt is sitting in the chair he always sits in, and this time Frankie is sitting in the chair I usually sit in because I'm not there. I'm in Jenny's basement, tongue deep in all that is holy about her. Maya is sitting in Frankie's chair. She's breathing hard, shaking, upset. She's saying things to Matt and Frankie about the messages she found and how she can't get hold of Patrick at all. When Maya mentions the prospect of Patrick and I together, something changes in Matt. He gets jealous.

This was something I never understood about what brought the whole thing down until now, just now when I'm telling you. When I said jealousy fucked things up at first, I meant that about Frankie. I thought it was about her, how she couldn't be honest about her feelings and how that made me better than her. The lack of honesty made everything spin out of control. I got too complacent in that, I got lazy. Honesty is hard. Matt pulled me closer to him and I let it happen. I wanted that. It was warm and easy.

Now that I sit here telling you this, this wreck that defined me for so long, I am laughing so hard. Because it's in this moment with the yellow light and the dust and Frankie sitting in my chair that she sees it so clearly on Matt's face. He's jealous.

Matt was jealous. He thought I was going behind *his* back, of all things, the sweet twist of a knife he thought was in someone else's back. Frankie saw the jealousy on his face like a stain, like the one I have lived with all these years, this mark, this curse of Cain, the fractured piece of shit heart they left me with. Lilith.

Jealousy is the admission to yourself that you are replaceable.

In that moment, Matt felt betrayed by what he thought was my lying, my perceived "unfaithfulness" to his irreplaceability.

Nothing lasts.

Maybe because Frankie had known him all those years, she could see his tics better than anyone else. She could feel it rise on the skin like electricity, see the hairs prick up on his forearms. Frankie could read it on his face. The kind of rage that burns so deep, a hole in the shape of *me* is left inside of him. He thought I was his and only his. I was no longer special Lilith but a common whore.

When Frankie called me that night, when she called over and over again and I didn't pick up, it must have confirmed for them some truth. Some alternate reality where everything was meant to happen exactly as it did.

THINGS WILL BE DIFFERENT THIS TIME AROUND

I SHOWED UP AT Matt and Frankie's to return Marilyn Manson's autobiography. Inside it, I placed a CD that I had burned a song onto—a song that I'd picked to encapsulate that entire year, just one. I picked this song to torture myself, because I liked the song a lot, and knew I would listen to it over and over again whenever I needed to be reminded what it felt like to hurt. The song was Nine Inch Nails' "With Teeth."

Matt opened the door and kept it close to his body and face, leaning out so I couldn't see inside. Frankie must have been home. I felt relieved that I did not have to face my fear of her somehow knowing all the wrongs we had committed, all the things we had done behind her back. *She just knows about the jealousy and that's it* I kept repeating to myself, over and over. After all, our transgressions weren't that bad. We kissed, we talked, we touched a little. It wasn't anything that hadn't been done before. It was only what happened inside of our bodies, the feeling centers, that had changed, and there was no possible way for her to know what was happening there. That part was under the skin, where she couldn't reach.

When Matt looked at me, I had to stop a smile from forming. He wasn't smiling and I did not want to come off as inappropriate. His mouth was terse and upset. The bags under his eyes were puffy, pronounced. His head was shaved clean again. I could hear the baby making noises somewhere in the apartment. The TV was blaring.

Matt sighed and I heard the clang of dishes in the background. The man might as well have been married. I started to pick my thumb bloody and wondered when one of us was going to speak. He just stared at me with this book in my hand and the first thing I could think of was what I always did, which was to make things worse.

"I didn't sleep with Patrick," I whispered. "I was with Jenny. I wish you would believe me."

He narrowed his eyes at me and then looked behind him. This man who fucked like a little dark god, who in my mind could have anything he wanted, looked back into the house like his mother would catch him doing something wrong. Mommy. The smell of rice and meat wafted out of the apartment and I had the realization I hadn't eaten anything cooked in weeks. I sniffed in the cold, waiting for an answer.

He put his hand out and I reacted by handing him the book, my finger in the spot where the CD was hidden. I let his finger slide into the open place when I handed it to him, and watched his eyes as he found the CD there. A tiny flash of recognition, another secret. We were silent. He nodded his understanding.

"You can't call the house anymore."

Matt closed the door until just a crack was left.

"I will call you when I can," he said.

Three days later, Jenny came into work with news. What was I hoping for? I didn't cook rice and meat. I didn't even think I could take care of myself, much less a child. Frankie did everything he needed her to. What would happen if we were together? Would I be the mother of Jett? My hobbies included touching myself, drinking cough syrup, and flirting with boys at RadioShack. Could I be anything else? I wondered if Matt had talked to Jenny and she'd smoothed everything out. Maybe he would finally call me. I could finally see him.

Instead, Jenny told me that Matt gave Frankie an engagement ring.

FROM TEETH

THOUGHTS OF MATT WERE an hourly fixation. My self-esteem was drying up without his attention, and as a result I spent an enormous amount of time trying to get Sam to sleep with me. He'd started dating someone, and this only made me want him more. I'd think about the movements Matt and I made with our bodies, sometimes I'd even think of Frankie, and since I could not have Matt in that moment I'd try, constantly, to come over to Sam's apartment so I could reenact my fantasies with him. If I closed my eyes, it didn't matter who I was blowing. I could pretend.

Sam took to fucking me on benches at local parks a few times a week. I wanted to be pushed further and further, and so we were doing more and more things that felt dangerous.

"Get naked," he'd say. I got naked. I did it because I knew whatever girl he was dating wouldn't strip in the middle of the night in a public park, and this was some kind of victory. I stood there, dropped my clothes onto the wet grass, and waited for his next command.

"Get on your knees," he'd say next. Everything he loved about me involved the shapes my mouth could make.

I'd blow him, and he'd come on my tits. I'd close my eyes when this happened and think of Matt, the warmth of it comforting me against the cold night breeze. Sam would say, "You like it when I come on your little tits, don't you." And I'd say yes. I'd use my shirt or dress to wipe up, and then we'd either fuck in the back of his Camaro or he'd drop me off at home.

What he always said about me, why I was such a slut, I had an itch I could never scratch. I'd never come, even with Matt or Frankie, yet I continuously pursued sexual relationships. Sam had never tried. Not until years later did he seem to care that much about making me feel good. Not until years later did he ask if I was falling in love with him.

After we fucked in the park, he'd drop me off, and then it was just me and my hands and body and a half-empty bottle of Robitussin writhing in the sheets. They say you have to know yourself and you will know your enemy. So I learned myself and the dark, uncontrollable wet spots on the sheets, rhythmic pulsing, waiting for something to happen that never did.

I think the fucking eventually got boring for Sam, so we took a walk around my apartment complex one night. For a moment it felt good to be physical in the world with a man without being in a bedroom. We flirted. Sam got sentimental and I told him to stop. We got back to the trailer, and he sat on the edge of my bed after my mom was well asleep. He told me to sit. I sat naked on his lap, moved my anchored legs until they burned. I didn't scratch the itch.

There were other men. One night I invited a high school ex over, the person I lost my virginity to. Another, Sam's roommate, hit me up when Sam was out of town.

I wondered if the same men were always coming back because even though I couldn't remember a single time they made me come, I still wanted them to come see me. Boy-I-lost-my-virginity-to moved back to the Springs and was dating a girl we both knew. I did the thing I always did, which was make a chaotic mess of his life. I played a game with myself, which was to see how sad I could make myself without his attention. It worked. His girlfriend worked on Thursday nights, and every Thursday night he'd come over, but we didn't speak on any other days.

My obsession with Matt began to lessen from an hourly occurrence to only daily. I got bored of being sexual when I felt like a dead package of skin waiting to be unwrapped. In my boredom I became impatient, so I started telling boy-I-lost-my-virginity-to what to do. I told him to put his mouth *there* so he puts his mouth there, because I was older than I was the day we first fucked, and in that moment I thought I knew what I wanted. His mouth stayed there and I grabbed his thick black hair and pushed his face into me. I felt the dark of my single room close in around us and questioned whether or not god was real, which I knew it wasn't, because I'd tried that trick before and I came up empty-handed.

The first time he fucked me wasn't the actual first time, but I'd since forgotten what he felt like, since I was only fourteen at the time. The other new thing was his interest in putting his thin fingers around my neck and pressing down, and I let him do it until the skin in my face burned hotter than my crotch. When he did this, I closed my eyes and thought of Matt again and only Matt, and waited for him to come.

Two months had passed since Matt left my life, and I slept through half the day, dreaming. In my dreams, Matt's hair was longer than it used to be, he was sweaty, heavy, his body ripe with fresh muscle. It was hard in that moment to imagine a world in which he could exist without me, but he laid me in a bed with dirty sheets and we fucked with most of our clothes on. The way he felt was safe and electric because it was that newness again that I was continuously chasing. He placed his thumb on the center of me; it was so easy for him to know where I needed to go. He didn't put his hand on my neck.

He put his hand on my head and directed me to kiss him. Our lips together created neon smears on my cheek, spit stuck to my neck, the crumpled clothes around my waist. His body like the Baphomet in Jenny's cards was a cage over me. This was how I liked for it to be.

Sam and I lay in the bed together, arms soothing each other's sides. He was a bottle of whiskey heavier on this night because his girlfriend had just left him. I was sober, surprisingly, because I worked early. I figured he called me because he was sad, or at least needed some validation. I was lonely and happy to oblige. On his back, he made the same snoring sounds my mother made, so I pushed his body hard until he rolled over, stuck in the drink and the sweat hot. I had never spent the night before but I didn't want to go home. The grey glow of a silent TV flickered at the foot of the bed. I played a game with myself.

"Stay still," I said, and I lay still.

I put headphones in, one ear open and one listening to a voice-mail on my phone. An old one left by Matt.

I counted the heartbeats in my head as I slowed my breathing down, sure not to twitch or move the mattress too hard. The game was that Sam couldn't find out, most likely wouldn't, his body exhaling whiskey dreams and heavyweight snores. He stirred, and I slowed down my circular motions until I was not moving at all. I tried to see how slow I could go until the rise came and I couldn't take it anymore, quiet and holding every muscle tight until it was gone, eyes tight shut with all the red of my body holding together. I let go, breathed, grey cold light still there.

THE SATANIC BIBLE SAYS MAN IS
THE MOST VICIOUS ANIMAL OF ALL

I SPENT THE BETTER part of spring fucking Jenny, getting lost in her body, and getting drunk. I felt bad that she would let me do this, especially after the tarot reading and the Tower card. I thought about the villain's fall from grace, how the card told me I needed to stop obsessing over Matt. After the reading, I became even more consumed by him. The smell of his skin was salt on the road. The color of his eyes was the tint over every other eye I saw. It overlaid the latent sadness in Jenny's eyes, the hot pink feel of her skin, it darkened the peeling paint of her basement bedroom. When Jenny's hands touched me, they were not hands anymore. They became objects with mechanical digits.

Jenny became an object in which I could place all of my feelings for Matt. I would see myself play fighting with her, our twin purple bruises yellowing out into our skin in little shark-teeth bite marks.

We both began drinking more. A fifth of Skol became a half gallon and soon we were killing one a night. I bit her harder. Drew blood from her skin seeking the taste of something else inside her, maybe Matt, or something to get me away from myself and into someone else. I bit her until the taste of her blood and cunt filled my mouth, spread across my tongue in thick mealy pulses of taste. Clouds of bruises dressed her stomach, neck, and arms.

Tonight we had something special, Monopolowa and Cherry Coke. We drank until the half gallon was near the end. I sat on the dryer and inhaled a cigarette out of the tiny window in her laundry room, letting the rush of post-sex pain take its course through me. I felt as though I was spending a lot of time acting upon Jenny rather than through her. I had been reduced to simple content. Rather than being seen as human, it was more as if I were a piece of entertainment to her, a block of text or commercial airspace which was mildly entertaining if only to fill out gaps in time. I couldn't be sure of her intentions any more than I could be sure of Matt's. His rejection of me was piercing through everything.

Jenny took my cigarette and took a drag. The rush wore off. She blew the smoke in my face and pushed me against the cold cement wall. Her lips met mine as the cigarette dragged against my arm, crushed between her body and mine.

"Ow!" I yelled. I pushed her off of me and slapped her before brushing flame off of my shirt and skin. I could feel the skin of my hand turn pink and burn a little, and my arm began to sear.

I was frustrated with her for hurting me, and for letting me hurt her. Her stupid Tower of Babel card, her stupid unwavering loyalty no matter how mean I was. She accepted my presence without question, and I could not determine what she really wanted from me. She made me feel like a predator. A meat eater. Like a pair of teeth with a stomach and no other purpose.

I pushed her again and jumped off the dryer. Jenny fell back and I laid on top of her, angry that she didn't want to fight back. I grabbed her chin in my hand and forced her to look at me, the tendons of her neck swallowing beneath my wrist. Her eyes, their thunderstorm color, squinted at me, but she didn't look scared. She smiled—she was playing. I pushed my hand harder into the thick chord of her trachea to see if her eyes would change and they did not. She moved her hips underneath me, so I bit her. She laughed and struggled a little, and twisted her wrists out of my hands, trying to push me off of her. I slapped her across the face again, harder this time. My palm buzzed. It must have scared the shit out of her because there on the floor, with me on top of her, she burst into tears.

"Fuck," I said. I watched her face go red and splotchy and immediately felt a wave of regret.

"Fuck, I'm so sorry." I spoke quietly, as if I were speaking to a baby or a dying animal. "You're okay," I said. I cradled her head in my hands and then kissed her. "I didn't mean to scare you. You're okay. I'm just drunk."

I said it over and over again, but she kept crying. In my gut was this deep, terminal feeling, like I might be executed for my terrible sins, for the things I did to her. I put my hands on her cheeks where the tears were, where her cheek was red. The numbness left my palm and it left my body.

Her crying made me cry. I cried until snot came out of my face and she stopped. She put her hands on my cheeks, slid them down to my neck and held them there. I could feel where her fingers passed the bruises on my neck, tender broken nerves making thin puddles of watercolor blood underneath. I leaned in to kiss her and where our lips met, there were tears and salt and snot. We kissed anyway, all of the gross things mixing and making slime on our cheeks. We kissed harder and kept our eyes closed. I focused on feeling what was inside of me. It used to be that each time I'd kiss a new person, excitement would spark my body to life. But I wasn't nervous anymore. I didn't get butterflies. I was kissing to be kissed, tongue and teeth and snot.

I traced my hands down her shirt and unbuttoned her pants. The light was still on and anyone who walked by on the street might see us there on the concrete floor. I tugged off her jeans, some Juicy Couture shit she bought at a thrift store. The hair on her thighs stood on end and all of her skin prickled from the cement.

Jenny watched me. She was a person who had to see as well as feel, maybe. I could navigate my life blind. All I cared about was seeking the next high. When she looked at me, it was different than how Matt saw me when he had the knife to my face. It was different that how Sam looked at me in his bathroom after the pool party. I watched it happen. Jenny disappeared. I watched a person disappear into the shell of another human, of me, in real time. Jenny seemed to leave herself and move into me.

My teeth no longer felt the need to devour, so I used my tongue instead to feel the parts of her that made her feel good. The parts that made her vulnerable. I kept my tongue on the fabric of her underwear and could feel her wet and my wet melt together through the lace. She grabbed my shoulders and pushed my face harder into her.

The way I ate her was like a meal, in little parts. Jenny gave small pieces of herself away each time my tongue pressed into her. A little less of her seemed to come back with me. The places where we became one thing together like this, our open membranes raw and bleeding. The cave of her colliding into my mouth, the place where words form. The way our darks connected. I didn't know what to think about how this felt other than we were here, alive and breathing and fucking, and maybe this was how it was supposed to be.

I took her to bed, laid her on her twin mattress, and placed the blanket over her. I wiped my face with a towel from her floor and slept on the mattress next to her, but on top of the blanket instead of under it.

The cigarette burn on my arm was not healing. I had been feeling slow, tired from the constant drinking every other night. If I was working, I was sober, but as soon as I was off the clock I was either with Jenny and drinking Skol, or in my room, snorting Vicodin and drinking any liquor that was in the house. I had taken to raiding the dusty cabinet underneath the china hutch in the living room while my mom was asleep. A few red wine bottles had vinegared, but I drank them anyway. A green, half-drunk bottle of shochu was in the corner collecting dust. It must have been my father's. A couple bottles of Johnny Walker Red. A bottle of Black Velvet. My mom must have forgotten these were here. The shochu was at least over twenty years old. I grabbed it and the Black Velvet and headed back to my room.

I turned the radio on my alarm clock to a classic rock station, which was currently on an AC/DC marathon, and lit a cigarette. I didn't have to work the next couple days, but Jenny was not returning my texts, so I took a swig of the shochu and chased it with an open bottle of sour red wine. My feet hung from the bed, and I kicked the trash underneath me, the empty plastic bottles of Robitussin and McCormicks juggling around dirtied paper plates and napkins, empty glasses crusted with rings of old cola.

I should've taken a break from seeing Jenny. She hadn't talked to me since our last drunk night, and I was getting paranoid. If she wouldn't reach out to me, I wanted to forget her and leave the whole thing behind before she could hurt me, too. I wouldn't have been surprised if she did hate me, if she wanted space. The more time I spent with myself, the more I found myself grotesquely annoying. My skin had been breaking out—from the constant drinking and my poor diet—and no makeup was covering it up. I wasn't showering much. My nails were dirty underneath, my legs unshaven. I could feel the oil built up in my hair and on my skin. I *was* gross. It was not a surprise that Matt no longer wanted to see me. I felt that I had peaked at eighteen, and nineteen was now just the slow slope downward. Right after high school, I had everything: good skin, shiny hair, a good body that liked to fuck. Right after that birthday, I had just started sleeping with my manager at work, and could add "fucked a boss" to my list of life to-dos. Sam seemed less interested in me now that I was nineteen and he was single. He was even scheduling me less at work, scheduling me at times when I wouldn't be around him. At nineteen, I did not feel Barely Legal anymore. Somehow, whatever power I thought I had with my body had already begun to fade. I knew women lost value as they aged, but didn't think I'd feel it so soon. I seemed to have wrinkles already, my body collecting scars. The bags under my eyes were getting worse. I wondered when I might start looking like my mother, acting like her, letting weight amass on my frame. We were both hiding in the same house with the same vices, a hole as big as a husband or father inside our ulcered, burning guts.

I lit another cigarette and picked at the scab on my arm, flinging the broken skin onto the trash heap of my floor. I didn't seem to feel the pain anymore. I took another drink of the shochu, bitter like rubbing alcohol, and wondered if I might go blind, before putting my cigarette out onto my forearm.

The pain was sharp and I breathed it in, like lightning illuminating a dark landscape. It was exciting to forget I hated myself so much. I rubbed the ashes off and watched as the broken skin bloomed from raw peach to dark red. Then everything was dull again.

THE MAN I COULDN'T MAKE INTO A GOD

I HADN'T HEARD FROM Matt or Frankie in about three months. One day after an early shift at work, my phone rang, a number I did not recognize. For a while after the breakup, I had obsessively checked my phone for missed calls from blocked numbers, as Matt would always call me without giving me a way to call him back. He seemed to enjoy that: being able to show up and disappear without repercussions blowing back on him. At this point, my obsession and my heartbreak had somewhat lessened, so I was surprised when I picked up the phone and heard his voice.

"I want to meet up," he said. His breath was hard. "I want to see you."

I was quiet for a second. A part of me felt angry. I had gone from thinking of him hourly to thinking of him only every other day or so, or when I felt particularly lonely, when it was quiet at night. Another part of me, the romantic in me, knew an opportunity like this would not come along again.

"When?" I asked.

"Right now."

I swallowed so hard I worried he could hear it.

"Frankie?"

"No," he said. "Just come over as soon as you can."

At home, I showered quickly, shaved my legs, ate a snack, and shit from my nerves. I paced in my bathroom, paced in the bedroom, back and across my full-length body mirror, staring at my skin in the sun. I grabbed a few pills from my mother's stash and set them on my nightstand. I put clothes on and took them off again, making a pile on my bed. I put on perfume. I applied makeup, took it off, frantically reapplied it, and then stood up, examining the foxglove tattoo on my thigh, seeing how it had healed, lotioned my legs, and put on a skirt. I tousled my hair so that curls came down either side of my neck.

When I got to the parking lot of his apartment, I checked my makeup again and got out of my car. He was already standing outside waiting for me, leaning against a wall. I was not prepared to see him, the way that he would look, and my nerves got to me. I realized I forgot my pills on my nightstand.

Matt smiled, all his teeth showing, cheeks pink from the wind. I hoped my holographic lip gloss sparkled in the sun as I walked. His freshly shaved head was like a goddamn peach. I wanted to devour him. I had forgotten how badly I wanted this, how much it hurt to look at him.

When I got closer, I noticed a cut on his left cheek.

"What happened to your face?"

"Frankie is doing an overnight," he said. "DV. She's in the tank."

I wondered if this was why he had spent so long ignoring me. He told me their fighting had gotten worse. She started getting physical, he said, and scared to retaliate, he just took it. If he tried to leave, she would block the door.

"Last night I couldn't anymore," he said. "She came at me with a broken glass. I grabbed her by the shoulders and shook her, just to make her stop."

"Jesus," I said.

"I just remember clenching my teeth and going *don't ever fucking touch me again*, and that must have scared the shit out of her, because she called the fucking cops on me. They showed up and I was the only one with physical evidence of abuse, so they took her. She was screaming a lot, and I kept telling her to stop resisting. The baby was crying. It was fucking chaos."

I stood for a moment looking at his eyes for any omission of truth. As gentle as he was with her, I had wondered this about men who held the monopoly on violence, what the response would be to a woman who was violent. It wasn't hard to envision Frankie there, in the hallway of their apartment, barking at him, flailing a broken piece of a glass she'd most likely thrown at a wall.

I was never taught that women were inherently weaker than men. I had learned it through sex, through Matt's fist at my neck. Men are taught to manipulate the world around them. Women are taught to manipulate men. I loved the violence of Matt, the pulse of it beneath the surface of his tranquil skin. It looked better on him. Frankie's violence was unrestrained. It was ugly. I knew this, and as a result I used it to my advantage.

"So she's just, like, in jail?" I asked. "Where's the baby?"

"Jett is at my mom's house. But yeah, they took her for a twenty-four-hour hold, I guess."

I leaned against him, could still feel the shower humid on his skin. His body tensed at first and then relaxed.

"Can you just come ride with me for a bit? Maybe spend the night?" he asked.

I feigned sympathy. I wasn't sure why I was there—did I like him anymore? After three months of torture without him? I looked at the slate-colored Malibu reflecting the old apartment buildings behind us, the abandoned church, the 7-Eleven across the empty parking lot. I felt more nervous than I had in a long time, which at least was something.

"Sure," I said.

When we walked to the car, I had this image of myself, separated from my experience. He got into the car first, and I tilted my hips as I went to sit down, the tattoo on the back of my thigh flashing *hopeless* before it made contact with the leather seat.

He pulled out of the parking lot and it hit me that this was the first time we were truly alone. An awkwardness rose in me, as if things had somehow changed and we were two new people on our way to some grand adventure, not the same ones that had been fucking in front of Frankie. I counted each breath down, reveling in the newness, placing my hand on his thigh and thinking, "This is the first time I am placing my hand on his thigh." The corners of my mouth pulled back and I thought, "This is the first smile I have shown him." We stopped at a red light and he glanced over, leaning in as if expecting a kiss. I leaned toward him and thought, "Perhaps I am the first woman after all." He smelled of beer and milk, his tongue soft like an animal in my mouth. His hand moved up my skirt and I felt reborn, my hands on the hard part of him. The novelty I chased, warm underneath his jeans. We stayed in this moment for what felt like a few minutes until a car horn blared behind us.

"Shit," he said. "Green light."

I laid back into my seat, my guts aching.

Our view was the curves and crags of a low green mountain and the road in front of us. I realized he was heading up to Gold Camp. I felt like his girl. Like we could still have been in high school. Gravel popped underneath his tires until we got to a pull-off section hidden by a portion of rock. I bit my lip, and he changed the CD out to the one I had slipped him in the returned book. NIN. I unbuttoned his pants, pretending I was the only girl to ever do it. My face this close, the smell of his sweat mixed with the air of everything else, the sour of his body and the cotton of his jeans.

I gave him head and thought about Frankie. I wondered what she was doing, what jail was like. This competition, like I was the one who was the mother of his child. *Daddy.*

His hands graced my upper back and that dissolving feel hit my shoulders and spread through the rest of my body. I emptied against his skin and let his presence permeate, making up for the months I hadn't seen him. Fucking or making love or neither, I didn't care anymore. The music in the car so loud it reverberated with harsh twangs. I thought about the way I grabbed Jenny, leaving marks in her skin. Matt sucked his lips and I bit them. I pulled on them with my teeth. I let go of his lip and kissed him again and pushed my tongue into my mouth, I tongued his teeth. He bit me back. I wanted to fuck him the way he had fucked me in front of Frankie. Hatefuck.

I traced my hands over his head. When he came to and looked at me, between our bodies where the heat was happening, something snapped. We stopped.

"Did you come?" I asked.

He nodded and pulled the condom off, looking for the tear. The car smelled heavysweet with the stench of wet latex. We both saw it at the same time, and he looked at me, throwing the condom and the wrapper out of the car window. He looked down and sighed.

Something fractured inside me. This crescendo was so disappointing. I didn't know how it happened. The car was the same. The road was the same. Matt was still the same person. But there was something that finally felt cold in me, a shutdown. When I looked at him, I saw that he had a woman, a kid, responsibilities. Things that I didn't care about or comprehend yet. He had places he was going to, a future. These were things I did not have.

We left Gold Camp. I traced my fingers along the leather edges of the seats in the Malibu, followed them up to the glove box. Matt looked over at me as I opened the glove box, papers, ice scraper, an old book injured with water. The heart I gave him was in there, underneath all the trash. It seemed appropriate to hide it underneath something so like myself.

Colorado Springs ascended before us as we hit Cheyenne Mountain Boulevard. Smoke curled up from the paper factory. I was reminded of the first time we rode up here, with Frankie, blasting Manson through the night with the dome light on. As we drove on, I looked in the backseat to see what I might look like if I were Frankie, staring back.

But I wasn't Frankie. I was Lilith.

He drove me back to his apartment building behind the highway barrier, and I stayed the night. His mother brought Jett back over. He mentioned needing to work in the morning. We went to bed early. I slept next to him, both of us alone. I texted Jenny throughout the night and had nightmares that Frankie would come home and find me there in the bed, that she'd drag me out by my feet. The phone kept vibrating with each text from Jenny, and I could tell it was keeping Matt awake, annoying him each time it happened. I finally fell asleep around 2 a.m.

We woke the next morning to his alarm. I felt groggy. The baby stirred, but we stayed in bed for a few long minutes and I tried to savor each part of the moment that I could—the smell and feel of his hair against my lips, the stubble that had grown in on his face overnight. I smiled at him, but he didn't smile back.

"You should get the morning after pill," he said. He wasn't sad when he said it. It was very matter-of-fact. "Frankie told me she wants to leave soon, but I can't fuck everything up right now."

I put my hand on his lips, felt the warmth. He turned his face away and I moved my hand to his. He did not respond.

"Frankie's leaving?" I asked.

"She threatened to move back to New Mexico," he said. "With her dad."

I stayed silent. I wanted to remember this exactly how it happened. In the light of the sun rising into the room, my free hand picked at the overlap between two small pieces of fabric in the blanket, a tiny thump against the mattress each time it gave way. I stared at my other hand on his face, which almost seemed detached from me. I could not feel his skin. I followed the squares of light with my eyes and then glanced at the alarm clock flashing green and blue. Frankie would be coming home.

"I'll go the pharmacy," I said. I lingered for a second before getting out of bed, stupidly waiting for an offer of money to pay for it, but he didn't make one.

MAN LOVED DARKNESS RATHER THAN THE LIGHT
BECAUSE HIS DEEDS ARE EVIL

I DECIDED TO WALK to the pharmacy. As I walked through the neighborhood, I sized up each house in my mind, their traditional 1950s ranch styling. One story. I tried to remember the home we lived in before my father died, but I only had remnants. A red door. Two steps down from the stoop. I remembered a giant sand pit in the back, a big yellow dog that had died when I was very young. The dog would dig deep holes into the sand pit, and I would crawl inside them, feeling hidden and safe.

The houses were old. An old woman on one side of the street came out from behind the back of her house on a gas-powered lawnmower, riding into her front yard. She waved at me and I smiled back, lifting my arm to shield my eyes from the sun. Another retiree on a lawnmower across the street. Having a lawn seemed like such a waste, but I fantasized about being able to have a garden. I imagined myself with Matt and wondered if he would be the type of person to mow the lawn once a week. If the stability of a lawn-care schedule was exciting or incredibly dull. Maybe, for the right kind of woman, lawn care was a noble act.

The sound of cars along Chelton drifted over the houses, reminding me that this was not a small suburban neighborhood, but part of a larger town of people doing things with their lives, making money. People who had places to be and things to do, unlike myself. I wondered, if I was the right kind of woman, if Matt would have

been less concerned about my becoming pregnant. The fear of it began to set in when I considered all of my failures and the freedoms I
was not ready to give up. I had nurtured my drug use as if it were a
baby and felt an infantile need to protect it. I often forgot to eat or
supplemented my caloric intake with beer. I had visions of a child
bursting out of my body, me alone in the wet and dark of it, a bleeding baby in a puddle with me. I was unable to nurture even myself,
still needed someone to take of me. Child rearing child. My obsessive
fears of aging kicked in, and I wondered how much worse I might
look after pregnancy, this big unknown, how I relied so intensely on
my body to get what I wanted. I saw how disinterested Matt seemed
in Frankie. Though he was tender with her, I suspected this was more
out of boredom than out of respect, but maybe I was wrong. Maybe
I was the wrong type of woman, the type that did not deserve to
be treated with such tenderness but with the full force of sexualized
violence, or a violence that men reserved for other men. I enjoyed so
much of the choking, the roughness between us, the bending myself
to please him, but also considered that I did not like myself. I could
not decide if the two situations, my hate for myself and my desire for
pain, were related. To be equal with others you have to add or sub-
tract from yourself, and I found myself unable to do either.

Maybe childbirth was the ultimate self-mutilation. If I did end
up pregnant and did not end it, I suspected Matt would not be there
for me and that I deserved that. Matt did not want to see what my
blood looked like if it also contained him.

These were the things I considered as I walked into the Wal-Mart
pharmacy at 9 a.m. on a Wednesday. The directions on the box said I
should prepare for period-like symptoms, and I was thankful to have
something like pain to look forward to. I sat on a curb in the parking
lot, debating what to do. Matt had said he wanted to be with me and
I wanted to trust it. But the caveat was this pill, a broken condom, a

question mark that could complicate things further. He only wanted me if I was hassle-free. I wanted to move out of this town, to pack up a car of belongings and leave with him, the way that he had claimed he wanted. But there was no evidence from his actions that this was anything but fantasy.

Yet, I still wanted to be complaisant. I did not want to complicate things if there was still a chance. I took the pill out of its blister package and chewed it up and swallowed it without water, licking the bitter pith off the backs of my molars.

My phone rang. Matt. I figured he was calling to check in on me.

"Hey," I said. "I got the stuff."

"Oh good," he said. "I was just calling to tell you that you are a filthy whore." I could hear the shape of the sneer in his mouth when he said this. It took me a few seconds to register that he was even speaking English because it was so unexpected.

"What?"

He didn't wait for me to speak but instead spoke over me and blurted everything out.

"You're a fucking whore and a home wrecker, L. You're disgusting. You will never be like Frankie."

I realized he was insulting me. Something pierced the very center of me and began to rip wide open.

"Okay, but—"

"This is one home you will never wreck, you fucking cunt."

There is a way people damage you, a way they'll change the structure of your DNA, the way your brain is wired. I stared at the concrete barrier ahead of me, landscaped trees, a wooden fence that divided Jenny's neighborhood from the Wal-Mart. A shaking began inside of me. It started small at first and then spread to my limbs until I was contracting every muscle in my body, pulling my neck taut and my mouth into a wide-open scream. The sound of my voice reverberated so loud I could hear my eardrums doubling back on themselves, something tearing inside my head. I threw my phone against the asphalt and it broke into three pieces—battery, back cover, and the phone itself scattered onto the street.

I thrashed my arms at my knees until my forearms burned numb. I ripped the scabs off of my body. Robitussin would be good right now, I thought. But instead I did what I always did, which was make things worse. I grabbed the phone, quickly put the battery back in and slid the cover on. I called back, but got only an answering machine.

"I just don't understand why," I said, and hung up.

I wiped snot on my shirt and tried to clean my face. I thought about closure. If he hated me, this meant it was all over. It meant no more waiting. It meant no more purgatory. I was free to leave, to get the fuck out of Colorado Springs without him shaping my life for the first time in months.

It was finally over.

I walked back into Wal-Mart to buy three bottles of cough syrup.

Back home, I was busy massaging my fucked-up face, naked in bed, when my scratched-up phone rang. It was from Matt and Frankie's house.

"Lilith," the voice said. "This is Frances."

My breath stopped and I waited, holding my stomach in my hands. The voice was the same business-like voice she used the first time we met. All the walls, everything I'd ever done to try and get to her, I failed. I had failed to make her love me, the way I'd failed to make anyone love me.

She must have come home from her overnight and found out about me staying the night. I ran through a list of the things I brought over, wondered if I had left any evidence of myself behind. I immediately guessed that Matt's call was him saving his own skin. She'd put him up to it, calling me names, telling me to stay away.

"You are a disgusting slut, okay?" she said. I nodded my head although she could not see it. Her voice was so flat, as if she were reading from a textbook. It echoed from the phone. The whole time she was putting up with me for the sake of her boyfriend, and now she had her chance to say what she'd wanted to all along. "If you ever come near my family again, I will fucking kill you."

The voice disappeared after that.

I stumbled into the hallway to get a glass of water, my mom drinking Seven and Seven in the living room. I peeked my head around to see if she was awake, which she was, barely. Maury Povich was playing on the TV. I walked quietly through the living room and entered her bedroom. I noticed the unmade bed, the dank smell, the smell of a body that smokes cigarettes and how nicotine sweats out of her pores into the sheets. In the corner, files tossed here and there on a desk, a vanity full of dusty jewelry boxes of unworn, expensive pieces. A couple of empty orange medicine bottles sat overturned on the nightstand next to an empty bottle of rosé.

I turned to the door of her bathroom and pushed it open, glancing down the hall to check for her stirring. The bathroom mirror, covered in toothpaste spittle, hadn't been cleaned in at least a year. The toilet was rust red inside, the water drained out from not being used. It was dark. The light shone through a small window. You could see dust caked onto everything. The toilet seat, the green countertops, the scale.

I walked over to the medicine cabinet; inside, three or four bottles of Percocet, Valium, and Vicodin. I took a few. Each bottle I moved revealed a ring of clean space underneath it, surrounded by an outer ring of grubby dust. After I grabbed a few tabs, I put each bottle back in its place like a puzzle piece.

On my way back to my bedroom, I grabbed a wine cooler from the kitchen, some pink shit. With the wine in one hand and the pills melting in the warmth of my palm, I threw myself on the bed and lay there for a second before setting everything up methodically on my desk. I closed the bedroom door and turned *The Golden Age of Grotesque* softly on repeat on the stereo. I watched the light fade out of my window and the window eventually turn black. I touched the sore spots of my body, the new scabs, the bruises Matt had left, the crescent-moon scars on my hip. Jenny's bite marks on my inner thighs. I spread my fingers over my fat labia, split like a rotting nectarine. My stomach was starting to cramp from the morning after pill.

I smashed my muscle relaxers on the desk with the butt end of a lighter, checked my phone to see if Matt had texted me. Nothing— not even a message from Jenny, or from Sam. I rolled Frankie's words over and over again in my head, imagined the words on her tongue. *I'll fucking kill you.* I felt like a common whore, someone's unwanted house cat. A home wrecker. If I had not pursued Matt alone, maybe it could have succeeded between the three of us. But my natural incli- nation was to lie and hide, and it felt good not to deny myself of that. People hide from the things that make them vulnerable while they wait for the right moment, the opportunity to prey. It is instinctual to live in the dark.

I separated the white dust into thin lines and grabbed a plastic straw from an old fast food cup on the floor. I cut the end off and looked inside, syrupy old soda crusted onto it, then sucked a line of powder into my nose. The middle of my face went harsh and dry and then burned softly as my sinuses expanded. I sniffed and waited for the emptiness to set in. I checked my phone again. It was four in the afternoon. Frankie might be making dinner right now, maybe Matt was silently fuming in the living room, if he was thinking of me at all. Sam would be at work. He hadn't responded to my texts in days. I wondered where Jenny might be.

I had the next two days off, with enough pills and enough Robitussin to bliss out for a while.

I clicked out a message letter by letter, then stared at my phone for a few minutes, deciding whether or not I should send it out. Too fucked up to determine whether the message was vulnerable or embarrassing, I deleted and rewrote it a few times. Another bump of Vicodin melted into the membrane of my nose. I sat back and thought about it more. Decided, fuck it. I addressed the text to Jenny. Then, finally, hit send.

i need you, it read.

come over.

ACKNOWLEDGMENTS

Thank you to Tom Spanbauer, Elizabeth Ellen, Amanda McNeil, Juliet Escoria, Rae Gouriand, Kirsten Larsen, Peter Derk, Kevin Meyer, Chelsea Laine Wells, Claire Vaye Watkins, and Asha Dore, without whom this book would not exist in its current form. To my co-editor at *Witch Craft Magazine*, Catch Business, who is the queen witch of proofreading. To my friends and family, who continue to support my writing even if they don't always "get it." Thank you to Jessica Martinez for being there through everything, to Bailey McKnight for the memories, and thank you to Kacy Dahl for being a bad Virgo bitch when I needed it most.

Lastly, thank you to my partner in life and crime, my husband.